WOMEN *of* MYTHOLOGY

WOMEN of MYTHOLOGY

KAY RETZLAFF

MetroBooks

MetroBooks

An Imprint of Friedman/Fairfax Publishers

©1999 by Michael Friedman Publishing Group, Inc.

Library of Congress Cataloging-in-Publication Data

Retzlaff, Kay.
    Women of mythology / Kay Retzlaff.
       p.   cm.
    Includes bibliographical references.
    ISBN 1-56799-757-0
    1. Women heroes—Mythology. 2. Goddesses. I. Title.
BL325.W65R47 1999
291.2´13—dc21   99-26787
                                         CIP

Editors: Celeste Sollod, Alexandra Bonfante-Warren
Art Director: Jeff Batzli
Designer: Milagros Sensat
Photography Editors: Amy Talluto, Erin Feller
Production Manager: Richela Fabian

Color separations by Spectrum Pte. Ltd.
Printed in Hong Kong by Sing Cheong Printing Co. Ltd.

10 9 8 7 6 5 4 3 2 1

For bulk purchases and special sales, please contact:
Friedman/Fairfax Publishers
Attention: Sales Department
15 West 26th Street
New York, NY 10010
212/685-6610 FAX 212/685-1307

Visit our website:
www.metrobooks.com

DEDICATION

This book is lovingly dedicated to Thomas Ross,
helpmate and wordsmith.

ACKNOWLEDGMENT

Special thanks to Tina, an Amazon for a new age.

CONTENTS

INTRODUCTION 10

Chapter I: SUMER 18

Chapter II: EGYPT 24

Chapter III: ANCIENT GREECE . . 38

Chapter IV: THE AMAZONS . . . 54

Chapter V: THE ROMAN
                 WORLD 82

Chapter VI: IRELAND. 104

Chapter VII: WARRIOR WOMEN
                 OF THE BIBLE . . . 124

Chapter VIII: CHINA 136

Chapter IX: JAPAN 150

Chapter X: INDIA 160

CONCLUSION 168

BIBLIOGRAPHY 172

INDEX 175

THE REALITY OF MYTH

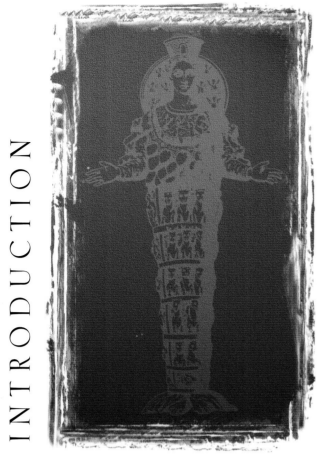

We often use the word "myth" to mean something that isn't real, but all cultures have created myths to express concerns—puzzles—that are deeply felt. Traditionally, myths answer questions: What is thunder? (The sky god is hurling thunderbolts.) Why do we have to work for a living? (Original sin.) Other times, myths are a way of asking questions, or trying to reconcile the seemingly irreconcilable. Myths about the power of women and men are the most resonant examples of these kinds of tales—right after those confronting the problem of good and evil.

One of the great questions is: How essential is the difference between women and men? How "hard-wired" are the differences in the way the sexes think and behave? Have things always been the way they are now? What beliefs best serve the community, in the opinion of the community's rulers? Who is telling the stories? Who is listening? Scholars believe that some of the great oral epics, such as *Gilgamesh*, the *Iliad*, and the *Odyssey*, were flexible. That is, the tellers had some leeway in adapting the tale, as long as they respected the ancient rhythms, the meter that made memorizing possible. The *Iliad* and *Odyssey*, for example, reveal layers of language from different periods and places. This process explains the changes in elements of the stories, including identities. In some Egyptian and Greek tales, the relations of characters

OPPOSITE: A fresco from the ruins of Stabia, destroyed by the eruption of Vesuvius in 79 C.E., portrays a graceful Diana, the Roman goddess of the hunt, with the bow and arrow that are her traditional attributes.
FOLLOWING PAGES: In Jacopo Tintoretto's sixteenth-century painting, the Roman Minerva, identifiable by her helmet, has challenged the prideful Arachne to a weaving contest.

BELOW: The Greek god-
dess Hera, protectress of
married women, here ritual-
ly sprinkles a diadem and a
peplos, or shawl, folded on
a table in front of her.
OPPOSITE: The Romans
called her Venus, the
Greeks, Aphrodite. Sandro
Botticelli captured a
Renaissance view of the
birth of the goddess of
love and beauty.

change drastically from version to version: a daughter in one retelling is a mother in another.

The stories reveal more profound shifts as well. Hera, in the Greek myths, is the wife of Zeus (whose name means "sky god"). Confronted with his philander-ing, she is resentful and vindictive, but, like many women, rather than standing up to her man, she punishes the "other" women and girls (themselves often the victims of rape or trickery) or their children by her husband. She is so vain that she carries a mortal—perhaps more accurately, an immortal—grudge against the human Paris for not electing her the most beautiful of

the goddesses, so the responsibility for the Trojan War is laid at her feet. Not much sisterhood there. Yet, the myths surrounding her reveal glimpses of another reality. Her name, the female equivalent of "hero," means "protectress," and a protector has the power. The earlier the source, the more beautiful and majestic she is; she is, after all, Zeus' sister as well as his wife. She watches over married women, and one of her daughters (and, thus, a version of herself) guards women in childbirth.

The Amazons constitute the classic image of power-ful women. Armed, battle-loving women, they were said to cut off one breast (their name means "without breasts") in order to wield their weapons more easily. In some tales they were man-haters, who coupled only to give birth, then kept only the girls, either returning the boys to their fathers, or, in the Greek way, exposing them to the elements to die.

Other myths reveal more fluid sexual roles. The Irish sagas, for example, tell of women whose desire is active and who, if they are queens, lead armies and generally carry on. Medb not only dallies outside her very friendly marriage (which seems merely to annoy King Ailill, her husband), but, determined to get what she wants, she is unself-consciously a pain in the neck. In this, she breaks two powerful late-twentieth-century taboos concerning acceptable womanly behavior.

In a number of cultures, going outside typical feminine behavior is not only acceptable, but praiseworthy, as long as it serves the community—meaning the status quo. Several Bible stories describe good women like Judith, who are courageous, clever, and self-sacrificing. When these women deploy their heroic qualitites for the good of their nation, they are good women. When, like Delilah, they are acting for the enemy, they are treacherous and trashy, misusing, even abusing, the power of their sexual attractiveness for ill.

In post–World War II America, many images were designed to lure Rosie the Riveter and her sisters home from the munitions factories. Women, the advertisements promised, could be girls again. In the 1950s and 1960s, many girls consciously and unconsciously gave up hopes of growing up to be anything but the lovable, endearingly inept object of a man's desire. In other words, they gave up their hopes of growing up.

In the movies, blonde women with little-girl voices— Doris Day (who was, as the phrase went, revirginized),

June Allyson, and Marilyn Monroe, among an army of others—always got their man. After marriage came American momhood, represented on television by impeccably groomed paragons such as the beautiful and baffled Donna Reed or the preternaturally wise Barbara Billingsley, mother of the Beaver.

Athena was the first woman warrior I learned about. As a child, I read all the encyclopedia entries I could find on the warrior goddesses. These images—so different from the limited roles seemingly available to women in the 1950s—excited my imagination. These mythical females of antiquity were active participants, prime movers in their worlds, enthralling visions of possibility for a girl in a society whose contemporary myths promoted femininity over womanliness.

The myths, legends, and tales in this collection reflect only some of the many stories of women war-riors that cultures all over the world have passed on through generations. Every myth has something true at its core—and many have history at their heart, such as the tales of Jingo Kogo. These stories were invented out of a common consciousness—or out of a collective unconscious, as some say. Each teller made each tale hers or his, choosing it because it resonated within the secret self, embellishing it to honor the tale and the magical, intimate act of telling.

Some stories were spoken for hundreds, even thou-sands of years before they were set down in cuneiform in clay, in hieroglyphics on ancient walls, on vellum and parchment in medieval monasteries. I have drawn these stories from original written sources, referring to at least two translations of each in order to find a core narrative.

It is my hope that these affirmations of female strength, in some cases harking back to some of the earliest human beliefs, will ring as true for you as they do for me—and as they have for generations of women and men of every place and time.

INTRODUCTION

SUMER

Writing began in the Fertile Crescent, the area between the Tigris and Euphrates rivers, in what today is Iraq, more than two thousand years before the birth of Christ. Inanna, the Sumerian goddess whose name means "Queen of Heaven," comes from this earliest known urban civilization. Although the various cities of the Sumerian civilization were thriving as early as 4000 B.C.E. (before the common era), the written myths that have come down to us are dated much later. There are sketchy materials that exist from as early as circa 2050 B.C.E., but the more detailed texts date from around 1900 to 1700 B.C.E.

Sumer was quite advanced technologically; for example, they had war chariots a thousand years before the Egyptians. The Sumerian influence is still present in our lives today, for they gave us a numbering system based on six. Thus, our days are 24 hours long, our hours have 60 minutes, our minutes have 60 seconds, and our circles have 360 degrees.

The Sumerians were the first to build temples. Their distinctive ziggurat structures led some scholars to speculate that the original inhabitants came from the mountains of eastern Iraq and that the pyramid-like structures were the Sumerians' attempt to replicate their mountainous homeland. The Sumerian civilization developed writing very early, primarily as a tool to record donations to the temple.

OPPOSITE: In the Babylonian *Epic of Gilgamesh*, one of the oldest of human tales, bird-footed, winged Lilith fled to the wild when Gilgamesh felled the Huluppu tree where she had been living.

Inanna is a moon goddess. She is called the First Daughter of the Moon, but she is also known as the Morning and Evening Star (the planet Venus). Her stories echo in part the lives of many women: in her youth, she is sought after by many suitors; as a young married woman, she gives birth to children; as an older woman, she is wise. As a goddess, she dies, descends to the underworld, and is reborn. Inanna is the virgin, matron, and crone par excellence. Her life cycle reflects that of the moon—waxing, full, and waning—and of the seasons.

Inanna's holy city was Uruk (known today as Warka), twelve miles (19km) from the Euphrates River, the middle of the Fertile Crescent. The location of the Garden of Eden was supposed to be between the Tigris and Euphrates rivers. Inanna walked in the garden.

Originally, each of the cities of Sumer had its own gods and goddesses. The cities, however, were always fighting over borders and water rights. The gods and goddesses of the victors gained those of the conquered, often merging with them. Inanna (known to later times as Ishtar) emerged victorious, dominating the other gods and goddesses. The story "Inanna and the God of Wisdom" illustrates her cleverness.

INANNA AND THE GOD OF WISDOM

Enki, the god of wisdom, the one who knows all, called his servant to him.

"Prepare butter cake. Pour cold water and beer," he said. "My daughter is coming."

Inanna entered Eridu, her father Enki's sacred city, with much pomp. On her head, she wore the crown of the steppe. She was tall and her hair was dark. Her eyes sparkled with laughter.

"I have come to sacred Eridu to honor the god of wisdom, Enki," she said.

"He has been expecting you," said the servant. "You are most welcome here."

Enki's servant led her to the holy table and gave her butter cake to eat. He poured cold water and beer for her to drink.

"Greetings, daughter," said Enki, the god of wisdom.

The servant refilled their cups with beer. They drank together in silence, and the servant never allowed their bronze cups to go dry. Enki raised his cup and offered a toast to Inanna.

"A blessing on you, daughter," said Enki. "I shall give you a triple gift, that of the high priestship, godship, and the crown of kingship itself."

Inanna raised her cup to the god Enki. She said, "I accept."

They drank some more, and Enki offered a second toast.

"A blessing on you, daughter," said Enki. "I shall give you another triple gift, namely that of truth, ascent and descent to the underworld, and the art of lovemaking."

Inanna raised her cup to the god Enki in thanks. She said, "I accept."

They drank more beer, and Enki offered yet a third toast.

"A blessing on you, daughter," said Enki. "I shall give you sorrow and joy and judgment."

Inanna raised her cup to the god Enki in thanks. She said, "I accept."

They continued to drink, and Enki continued to give Inanna his blessings. She accepted them all, giving her father thanks each time.

In addition to his previous gifts, Enki, the god of wisdom, gave his daughter the gifts of music, of waging war and plundering cities, of heroism and power, of creating strife and of soothing words that calmed strife. He gave her, too, the ability to bless families with the gift of children and power over all the arts of humankind.

At the end of the evening, Enki called his servant to him. "See the young lady out," he said. "Make certain she and all the gifts that I have bestowed upon her safely reach the city of Uruk."

"Yes, lord," said the servant, and he escorted Inanna to the dock where her boat, the Boat of Heaven, was anchored. He helped her load her precious cargo and watched as the boat left the dock, setting sail for Uruk, the holy city of Inanna.

The next morning, Enki arose, groggy with the beer of the night. When his head had cleared, he looked for his great treasures, but they were nowhere to be seen. He searched Eridu, his city, but his great gifts were gone.

"Servant!" he yelled, "come here at once!"

His servant came to him.

"Where are my precious things? The priesthood? Godship? Kingship? Heroism? Power? Where have they gone?"

"You gave them to the young lady, your daughter, Inanna," said the servant.

"Where is she now?" demanded Enki.

"She has sailed for Uruk on the Boat of Heaven," said the servant.

"Bring her back," commanded Enki. "Bring her back at once."

"She nears her own city," said the servant.

"How can I stop her?" Enki called to him the enkum, hairy creatures that can fly through the air.

"Bear my servant to my daughter Inanna on the Boat of Heaven. Bring them back to me," commanded Enki.

So along with Enki's servant, the enkum sped to the Boat of Heaven. From the deck of the boat, Inanna stood looking at her city, whose dock was only a few feet away. Waiting on the quay was Inanna's entourage, led by her faithful servant Ninshubur, the woman warrior.

"Your father, the god of wisdom, most urgently commands that you return with his precious gifts to Eridu, and restore them to him." said the servant of Enki. "He must be obeyed."

"He breaks faith with me," said Inanna. "My father gave me the precious gifts. He has lied. I will not return."

At that, the enkum seized the Boat of Heaven and began the return journey to Eridu.

"Help me, Ninshubur!" commanded Inanna. "My faithful warrior, save me!"

Ninshubur screamed and shattered the air with her hand. The blow sent the enkum tumbling through the air, all the way back to Eridu.

But the god of wisdom wasn't so easily bested. He commanded his giants to reach down and capture the Boat of Heaven. Ninshubur pulled the Boat of Heaven free from their grasp. The god of wisdom then commanded his sea monsters to seize the boat from below, but Ninshubur wrested it from their jaws.

Ninshubur fought bravely and hard, and overcame each of Enki's attempts to take back the things that he had given to Inanna. At last, the victorious Ninshubur greeted the Boat of Heaven as it entered the sacred gate of the city of Uruk.

"You are safe within the city of Uruk, my lady," said Ninshubur.

"Let there be joy and celebration in the city," said Inanna, "for I bring the gifts of my father Enki."

In the meantime, Enki called his servant, "Where are my precious gifts?"

"The lady Inanna has already gone to deliver them to the sacred temple of Uruk," said the servant. "She is even now presenting them to the people of Uruk."

"Very well," said Enki. "Let my daughter keep what I gave her. After all, her city and my city are allies."

Inanna happily showed the people of Uruk all the wonderful gifts that the god of wisdom had bestowed upon her. In celebration, the people danced and sang in the streets, and Enki, the god of wisdom, pronounced a blessing on the people of Uruk, wishing them all prosperity and joy.

OPPOSITE: This alabaster statuette from Sumer, showing a woman holding a vase, may date to the fifth century B.C.E. ABOVE: A detail from a third-century B.C.E. Sumerian panel from Ur shows what may be a victorious army. The figures are of engraved shell; the background is lapis lazuli.

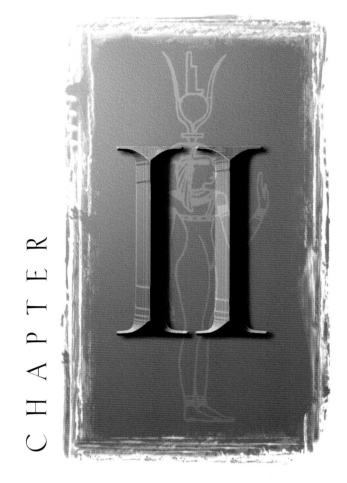

CHAPTER II

EGYPT

An Egyptian culture existed as early as 4500 B.C.E. Writing spread from the Fertile Crescent to Egypt in the twenty-eighth century B.C.E., around the time that the pharaoh Menes consolidated Upper and Lower Egypt, creating the first Egyptian dynasty. With political unification, some of the many gods and goddesses of both kingdoms faded, while the roles of others merged.

The story "The Wrath of Re" tells of a conflict among the gods. Isis tricks Re into revealing his secret name—the one given him at birth by his parents—thereby giving her power over him. (Isis is older than Re, and she resents the pompous upstart, which is the reason for her underhanded actions.)

With the unification of Egypt, Isis, like many of the popular gods and goddesses, took over the roles of others. She is one of several goddesses who act as manifestations of one another. One of her personifications is Satet, a rain goddess who is depicted carrying a bow and arrows. In this, Isis resembles Neith, a rain goddess of possibly Libyan origins, who also carries a bow and arrows, symbolizing lightning.

One of the oldest goddesses of Egypt, Neith, the mother of all the gods and goddesses, is the cow who gave birth to Re. During the dynastic period, Neith was so popular that every important local

OPPOSITE: Hathor, the Egyptian queen of heaven, was sometimes depicted as a cow. At Re's bidding, she destroyed humankind. Hathor was also identified with Sekhmet, the goddess of war. The wife or mother of Horus, her name can be interpreted to mean "home of Horus."

goddess was identified with her. As the Lady of the West, the direction in which the sun sets, she is the death goddess, who oversees the weighing of the words of the dead; she is also a goddess of the underworld. Thus Neith both gives life and takes it. Neith is also the great watery void that gave birth to Re. Part of Neith's role is to oversee the annual flooding of the Nile, the great river that makes agriculture—and therefore life—possible in the region. In this capacity, Neith brings celestial food to the world. She is also the goddess of war. (In these attributes, Neith closely resembles the Sumerian goddess Inanna.) So thoroughly were Isis and Neith identified with each other that both were celebrated at the annual Feast of Lamps, according to the Greek historian Herodotus.

Like the gods and goddesses of ancient Sumer, those of Egypt had their own cities. Neith's holy city was Sais, located in northern Egypt.

The head and horns of a cow were Neith's symbols. Hathor, who becomes the Eye of Re in the story "The Wrath of Re," was originally the deity of the city of Dendera, where she also had the form of a cow. Thus, Neith and Hathor have a great deal in common, and in later times they actually merged in myths such as "The Wrath of Re."

THE WRATH OF RE

As a young god, Re, the sun, fought hard for supremacy over the gods of Egypt. After much struggle, he managed to subdue his enemies, and he made hostages of their children. His reign was a time of peace and prosperity for the gods and the people of Egypt. But, as do all things, Re grew old. There came a time when he could no longer keep rebellion at bay.

Isis, the great goddess from before the time of Re, plotted against him. She knew many things, but she did not know his secret name, the name that gave Re power. She watched and waited, following him.

As old men will do, Re often had to clear his throat, and he wheezed when he breathed. One day, Re cleared his throat and spat on the earth. Isis knelt and kneaded the spittle and the earth together, making a snake of the clay. She made it as long and as poisonous as a spear, then threw the writhing snake on the path where Re often walked.

The next day, as Re walked with Pharaoh and those who serve the gods, he stepped on the snake, which bit him. Re screamed in pain. As the poison spread through his body, Re became mute with fear.

"What is it, my lord?" asked an attendant, but Re had no voice to answer him.

The poison spread quickly, and Re's body shook with agony. At last, Re calmed himself enough to speak to his attendants.

Isis watched from a hiding place.

"A poisonous snake has attacked me," said Re. "Nothing has ever hurt like this before. Bring the all-knowing gods to me that they may cure me and take away this horrible pain."

The gods came at the command of Re. Isis, known far and wide for her wisdom and her ability to heal, came too.

"What is it, divine Re? How may I serve you?" asked Isis, never letting on that she was responsible for Re's pain.

EGYPT

"A snake has bitten me while I walked," said Re. "Take this pain from me. I burn, yet I shake with cold. Water pours from me, and my eyes won't focus. I can't see the sky."

"Perhaps I can help, divine Re," said Isis charmingly, "but if I am to do so, you must tell me your secret name."

"This can't be," said Re. "My father and mother told me my secret name upon my birth. They told me never to tell another my name, for if I did so, evil magicians might use the power of my name against me."

"I can't help you, divine Re," insisted Isis. "Without the power of your name, I can't take away the pain."

"How dare you!" said Re. "Do you know who I am? I created heaven and earth. When I open my eyes, the sun shines. When I close my eyes, night covers the earth. I command the waters of the Nile to flow. I make time itself. Not even the gods can know my sacred name."

The poison crept through his veins like a flame, burning his flesh and searing his very breath. He cried out in pain.

"I can't help you unless you yield your sacred name to me," said Isis.

She turned as if to go.

EGYPT

"Very well," said Re, and he whispered his name to her. The great goddess used her magic to heal Re, but the god never fully recovered his strength after the serpent's sting. He had become frail and feeble. Even puny humans laughed at him in his old age.

"Look," they said. "He is nothing but gold and silver and lapis lazuli. These are only statues of Re. Surely he no longer exists."

Their words stung Re nearly as much as the viper's bite. Anger filled him.

"Bring the old gods to me," he commanded. "Bring to me my right hand, the very eye of my crown, the goddess Hathor."

All the old gods and goddesses came at Re's command. They knelt in his presence and asked him what it was he needed.

"You gave me birth," said Re. "I need your counsel now. I trust you to speak the truth. Humans plot against me, ancient ones. What shall I do? I determined not to destroy them until after I had talked to you."

The most ancient god, Nun, the primeval ocean, spoke. "Send the goddess Hathor to kill those who speak evil of you."

Re's right hand, Hathor, the ancient goddess, stood straighter at the mention of her name. Her dark brown eyes glowed with an inner fire. The headdress that she wore, cow horns supporting the disk of the full moon, shone like gold.

The ancient gods and goddesses murmured their agreement.

"Go, then, Hathor," said Re. "Punish those who laugh at me."

"I will subject and destroy those who laugh at the power of Re," said Hathor.

"Subject them," said Re, "and in return I will give you the name Sekhmet, goddess of war."

As evening descended upon the earth, Hathor went down to the earth in the form of a great cow and began destroying the humans who had laughed at the power of Re. People ran

LEFT: Horus, the hawk-headed god, leads a timeless procession. Behind him, the eternally youthful Hathor bears the full moon between stylized cow horns. Her hand raised in praise or blessing, she salutes Horus, in some tales her husband, and in others her son.

which flowed upon the earth, and the beer. As evening descended, Re commanded that the mixture be poured upon the fields of Egypt, so that Hathor might find the earth flooded at dawn's light.

The next morning, Hathor waded through the inundated fields of Egypt, admiring her reflection in the blood-red liquid. She drank deeply of the "blood" and soon became drunk. At last, sated, Hathor could hear the messengers of Re calling for her to return to Re's side.

"Well done, eye of my crown," said Re. "You have taught the humans a lesson they will not soon forget."

"Thank you," said Hathor.

"I am weary of humans," sighed Re. "They play great havoc with my emotions. I think, perhaps, that it is time for a younger god to deal with them. I need to rest. I will go and sit upon the back of the splendid Cow of Heaven."

There were whispers among the gods and goddesses, each wondering which of them would be placed in charge of human affairs.

"I have decided the god of wisdom, Thoth, will be my deputy upon earth," said Re.

"Thank you," said Thoth. "I will do my best to serve you."

"You must, however, take care not to step on snakes," said Re, "They are dangerous beings."

from her terrible wrath, fleeing for the mountains and up the river. Entire towns ran with blood. At dawn's light, Re looked down upon the carnage that Hathor had wreaked in his name, and pity began to dull his anger. He sent messengers to Hathor, but she was filled with blood lust and heard them not.

"Hathor hasn't drunk her fill of the blood of humans," said Re. "I must hurry if I am to save any of these poor creatures."

Re commanded his messengers to bring red fruit to give to the god Sektet to make into juice. Re commanded his slaves to crush barley and to brew beer. He then mixed the red fruit, some of the blood from the humans

ANCIENT GREECE

The three major Greek warrior goddesses—Athena, Hera, and Artemis—predate even Athens. Their roots can be traced to the island of Crete, where Athena was a protectress of home and town, and Hera and Artemis were worshiped in forms other than their Olympian manifestations. Minoan and Mycenaean seal stones, dating to about 1500 B.C.E., depict the roles of the goddesses. Stories about them, and about the other Olympians, the deities composing the Greek Pantheon, are later found in Homer's *Iliad* and *Odyssey*, the oldest works of Greek literature, composed around 800 B.C.E.

Athena and Hera, who share a long and close relationship, are the preeminent warrior goddesses of ancient Greece. Athena, who always carries a spear, often enters the thickest part of battles, as do her male counterparts, Apollo and Ares. Hera, besides being Zeus' wife and older sister, is a charioteer. The goddess Artemis, huntress and mistress of animals, carries a bow and arrows.

Male gods attempt to thwart Athena's power, but the wily goddess is not easily subdued. Zeus, Athena's father, swallowed her mother, Metis ("Wisdom"), to prevent their child's birth, but Athena persisted in being born, issuing full-grown and fully armed from her father's forehead (he got a very bad headache). However, according to the male writers who orchestrated her affiliations, Athena

OPPOSITE: Not a chorus line, but three goddesses, Hera, Athena, and Aphrodite, vying to be elected the most beautiful by the Trojan shepherd Paris. They all attempted to bribe the judge, but the goddess of love won out.

turns her back on femininity because masculinity is more powerful. Athena spends time with Hera, but mostly she remains outside the community of Olympus. In the *Odyssey* she spends most of her time interacting with humans, such as Odysseus.

Athena also nurtures young men to adulthood. She has a close relationship with Herakles, as depicted by artwork from as early as the sixth century B.C.E. In addition to her more militant duties, such as inventing war chariots and ships, Athena gave Athens the olive tree, and oversees womanly arts, such as spinning, weaving, and embroidery. Besides being a warrior, Athena is regarded as a goddess of wisdom and a protectress of archi-tects, sculptors, and potters. Somewhere in her ancient his-tory, she may have been connected to the cycles of fertility and renewal of the land, like the Egyptian goddess Isis and the Sumerian goddess Inanna.

In the *Iliad*, Hera, the chario-teer, handles horses well. Once a

great goddess, she was in later times demot-ed to Zeus' surly wife, who seeks every opportunity to thwart his adulterous plans. Homer refers to Hera as "ox-eyed," tying her, at least thematically, to Hathor, the cow goddess of Egypt. Hera's temple at Samos was the largest shrine in Greece.

The stories of these goddesses show, as in the Egyptian story of "The Wrath of Re," a converging of matriarchal and patriarchal traditions, in which the goddesses' roles have been usurped by male deities. However, despite the gods, the goddesses manage to take their rightful roles in shaping the history of the Greeks. Their active parts in the most consequential war of ancient times are portrayed in "Athena and Hera: The Trojan War."

ATHENA AND HERA: THE TROJAN WAR

During the great war between the city of Troy and the men of Greece, Achilles, the Greek hero, became angry with Agamemnon, the leader of the Greek forces, over a question of honor. This could not have come at a worse time: Achilles had been leading the fight against the Trojans, and without him in the battle, the Trojans would gain the advantage.

At the same time, Zeus, the king of the gods, had to work hard to keep the gods and goddesses of Olympus from interfering in the war, since the deities had taken sides. Hera, Zeus' wife, and Athena, his war-loving daughter, sided with the Greeks. Apollo and Aphrodite allied with the Trojans. In truth, Zeus himself sided with the Trojans, but in order to keep peace on Olympus, he decreed that none of the gods, including himself, should get involved.

However, Agamemnon had committed an outrage against divine Apollo when he captured Chryseis, the Trojan daughter of Apollo's priest, and then refused to ransom the girl back to her father as was customary. The priest, in sorrow and anger, prayed to Apollo, seeking revenge for this insult.

ABOVE: Delphi, one of the most sacred places of antiquity, was the site of the Pythic oracle of Apollo, famous throughout the Mediterranean. Three columns remain of the fourth-century B.C.E. sanctuary of Athena Pronaia.

LEFT: Athena brought civilization to humankind. Among her gifts are olive trees, weaving, and justice and skill in war. Here, Athena does not wear her body armor, for she mourns, supporting herself on her golden staff.

OPPOSITE TOP: This fifth-century B.C.E. drinking bowl shows Athena beautifying herself for the judgment of Paris.

OPPOSITE BOTTOM: A scene from the Trojan War: Athena oversees two Greek warriors drawing lots for the arms and armor of the slain Achilles.

To punish the Greeks, Apollo shot plague-carrying arrows into their ranks. Achilles urged Agamemnon to undo his sin by returning the priest's daughter to the Trojans. The other Greeks agreed with Achilles, and Agamemnon was forced to relinquish his prize.

In retaliation, the angry Agamemnon took Briseis, the Trojan girl Achilles had been given as booty. Sulking, Achilles retired to his tent and called out to his mother, the sea nymph Thetis, informing her of the wrong that had been done to him. He asked her to intercede on his behalf with Zeus, king of the gods on Mount Olympus.

Thetis flew to Olympus and threw herself at the feet of Zeus.

"Oh, great Zeus," she wept. "My son, Achilles, has been greatly wronged by Agamemnon, leader of the Greeks. Agamemnon has taken Achilles' prize, the lovely Briseis, who had been given to him for his valor in battle."

"What do you wish me to do?" asked Zeus.

"Punish the Greeks, great Zeus. Show them what it means when they wrong a great man."

"You know, sweet Thetis, that I have had to work hard to keep the gods and goddesses, especially that hot-headed wife of mine, Hera, out of this human fray," said Zeus. "How would it look if the king of the gods broke his own rule?"

"But my son has been made to suffer for his service to the gods, great Zeus," said Thetis. "My son, Achilles, sought relief from Apollo's arrows of sickness. Apollo was angry because the Greeks had disgraced his priest."

"Tell me more," said Zeus.

So Thetis told Zeus of Agamemnon's evil treatment of the priest and of Achilles' counsel to return the captured girl.

"Achilles urged the Greeks to return the priest's daughter," said Thetis. "Surely, Achilles did honor all of Olympus in this regard."

"This was indeed an honorable thing to do," said Zeus.

"Agamemnon returned the priest's daughter," said Thetis, "but, in spite, he has taken Achilles' prize for himself. At this blow to his honor, Achilles took his men to their ship and refuses to take part in the fighting."

Zeus thought to himself that without Achilles in the battle, the Trojans would have the upper hand. Thus, his favored city could overcome the Greeks, and he would not have to do much. All he had to do was make sure that Hera did not come to the aid of the Greeks. If Hera were to find out that he supported the Trojans, from sheer obstinacy she would take a more active role in backing the Greeks.

Zeus was pleased to have the beautiful Thetis grasping his knees in supplication. He patted her affectionately on the head, then looked around to make sure Hera wasn't looking. Even though he was king of the gods, Hera could make his life miserable. She didn't approve of his relationships with the younger goddesses.

"My dear Thetis," said Zeus. "I'm pleased that you've come to me. What can I do to help you in your distress?"

Thetis wept more loudly and grasped his knees more tightly. "Punish the Greeks, great Zeus. Let the Trojans drive them back to their ships. Show them that they shouldn't have slighted my heroic son."

"That I can do," said Zeus, whispering lest Hera or the other gods overhear. Zeus was pleased with himself, for now he had the chance to help his beloved Trojans, as well as the beautiful Thetis.

"Anything you can do, great Zeus, will be greatly appreciated," Thetis whispered, looking up at Zeus through misty eyes.

"Whatever you do," said Zeus, thinking he had never seen anything lovelier than Thetis' tear-stained face, "don't tell a soul about our plans. You know

Hera. She takes delight in opposing me in everything, so if she finds out, she will take it upon herself to thwart us."

Zeus called the gods and goddesses together in the great banqueting hall of Mount Olympus to discuss the affairs of the men below.

"So, what do you think about this affair between the men of Greece and Troy?" he asked. Everyone started to talk at once, each praising the virtues of the warrior she or he loved best. Amid the hubbub, they reached for their cups, which were filled with nectar, and toasted one another.

Except for Hera. She didn't drink, but instead looked at Zeus, her large, dark brown eyes full of suspicion. Zeus avoided her gaze, which made her suspect her husband even more.

LEFT: A frieze on the Parthenon, one of the finest of ancient Greek monuments, dedicated to Athena the Virgin, shows Poseidon, the god of the sea; Apollo, the god of the sun, music and poetry, prophecy, and healing; and his twin sister, Artemis, the chaste moon goddess and mistress of the hunt.

"What have you been up to, you old goat?" she said.

"Whatever do you mean, you crazy old woman?" said Zeus.

"Crazy, am I?" said Hera. "I know that look. I've seen it often enough before. What sweet young thing has been clasping your knees?"

The room became very still. The gods and goddesses looked at one another, uncomfortable with the argument. All stared at the faces of the goddesses one by one to see who would blush.

Hoping to launch a counteroffensive, Zeus spoke to all. "As you know, my war-loving daughter Athena and my ever-quarreling wife Hera support Menelaus the Greek."

"Surely you aren't too embarrassed to tell us what scheme you've been hatching," said Hera. "Have you decided to break your own rule and take sides, helping your beloved Trojans?"

"Silence, Hera. I am the king of the gods. Don't expect to know everything I know," said Zeus.

"You don't have to tell me anything," said Hera. "I saw that nymph Thetis flitting about this morning. It's obvious that the two of you have been plotting together to help that petulant brat of hers. You've decided to let the Trojans overrun the Greek ships, haven't you? Just so the childish Achilles can prove to the Greeks that they need him. You've been looking for an excuse to help your precious Trojans get the upper hand. Why don't you admit it?"

"That's enough!" Zeus thundered.

Hera leaned back in her chair, suddenly silent, her face drained of color. She opened her mouth to continue, but her son Hephaistos shook his head. The great goddess closed her mouth and stared at her brimming cup. There was a heavy, awkward silence throughout the banquet hall. The clunk of a log on the fire seemed as loud as a thunderclap; the gods and goddesses were startled. The vast hall remained quiet until Hephaistos started bustling about, refilling cups with nectar and cracking jokes. Soon, the sound of laughter filled the hall. Only Zeus and Hera remained silent, their handsome faces pale.

At last Zeus drank from his cup, and his good humor returned soon thereafter.

Hera turned to Athena at her side. She asked, "How shall we undo this treachery?"

"It would not be too difficult to rally our beloved Greeks," said Athena.

"Then, gray-eyed Athena, let us visit the battlefield," said Hera, "and see what we can do there."

On the plains of Troy, the Trojans easily pushed the Greeks, without their hero Achilles, back toward the ships. Night fell and both sides pulled back.

Emissaries went out to discuss a truce, for nine years of war were taking their toll on both sides. The Greeks wanted to go back home. The Trojans wished them there.

Athena eagerly pulled on her aegis, her armored breast-plate, and sped from Olympus to the plains of Troy. She took on the appearance of a Trojan warrior and stood in the Trojan ranks, watching the Greeks drawn up in their camp, both sides observing the truce.

"You know," said Athena to a Trojan warrior, "the Trojan who took it upon himself with steady aim to kill Menelaus with an arrow would be a hero forever. Paris, prince of the Trojans, would probably make that man very wealthy indeed."

"The arrow would have to fly true," said the man.

"Can't Apollo, the god of archers, help with such a feat?" asked Athena, in her disguise. "A heartfelt prayer wouldn't go unanswered. A promise to sacrifice a lamb would help."

The warrior prayed to Apollo, promised the sacrifice of a lamb, strung his bow, and picked a brand new arrow from his quiver. He prayed as he pulled the bowstring back and let the arrow fly. Athena, taking on the guise of a Greek warrior, then sped to the side of her favorite, Menelaus, just as the arrow was about to strike. She guided the arrow to Menelaus' belt buckle, where it struck the metal and went through three layers of leather and his leather apron, drawing blood, but not seriously wounding him.

Warriors on both sides raised a great shout, and the battle resumed. Many died. Ares, the god of war, worked the Trojans into a battle frenzy, and Athena rallied the Greeks. At last, Athena went to Ares' side and put a hand on his arm. "Let's sit this out," she said. "We have done our work. Now let's see who Zeus chooses as victor."

Ares joined Athena on the riverbank, and from this shaded spot they watched as the battle raged. However, the gods and goddesses of Olympus flew to the battlefield, each giving aid to her or his favorite warrior. Even the goddess of love, powerful Aphrodite, hovered over the battlefield, trying to protect her Trojan son, Aeneas.

Not for long could war-loving Athena keep from the din. She swept into battle to aid the Greek warrior Diomedes, granting him the privilege of being able to see the Olympians. "I've refreshed you, Diomedes," Athena told the warrior. "And I've given you the ability

OPPOSITE: Many-breasted Artemis of Ephesus reveals her Asian origins as a fertility goddess. ABOVE: Greek goddesses were often as lustful as their male counterparts, as exemplified by Eos' pursuit of Kephalos, son of Hermes.

to see the immortals on the field. Don't fight against any of those from Olympus, except for that fool Aphrodite, daughter of Zeus. You may wound her, but her alone."

Diomedes could see Aphrodite on the battlefield thanks to Athena's gift, and he struck at the hand of the goddess of love with his spear, tearing her palm so that the ichor, the immortals' blood, ran out. She screamed, then seeing Ares sitting on the green riverbank, his horses and chariot beside him, she fled to him.

"Brother, let me borrow your horses. I'm in great pain," Aphrodite said, showing her wounded hand to Ares.

"Take the horses," he said. The goddess Iris took the reins and acted as charioteer. Athena followed behind to see the fun. The three goddesses flew to Olympus.

In the meantime, Diomedes strove to kill Aeneas, even after Apollo took him under his protection. Apollo spied Ares sitting on the riverbank.

"Are you just going to sit there?" he yelled over the din. "Get this man Diomedes off me. Do something."

Ares reentered the fray, going among the Trojans and rallying their flagging spirits. Finally, Apollo was able to take Aeneas away from the battlefield.

Hera watched from Mount Olympus and became distraught that the Trojans were fighting back. She called Athena to her. "This will not do," she said. "We must hurry to the battle."

Hera went to harness her horses. Hebe, the cup-bearer of the gods, fetched the chariot, which was a sight to behold. The wheels were made of bronze, the sides were of woven silver, and the chariot floor and the horses' harness were crafted from the finest gold.

Athena put on her armor, strapping on the aegis and placing her golden helmet on her head. In her hand she carried her long spear.

Hera urged the horses through the gates of Olympus. Zeus sat on a hilltop nearby. Hera pulled up on the reins and stopped beside him.

"I thought the Trojans' cause was their own. Have you taken sides?" she asked. "Would you be upset if I taught Ares a lesson?"

"Not at all," said Zeus. "Let Athena deal with Ares."

Hera and Athena joined the fighting at its thickest, near those who fought to defend Diomedes, who had dropped from the battle. He was cleaning a wound when Athena appeared to him.

"What are you doing here, out of the battle?" asked Athena.

"Following your instructions, mistress," said Diomedes. "You commanded me not to wage war against the immortals. It's obvious that Ares is responsible for the Trojans retaking the field."

"Well done," said Athena, "but it's time to reenter the battle. Leave Ares to me." She filled Diomedes with renewed vigor, and he rejoined the battle.

Athena made herself invisible. Ares, the god who inspires the blood-lust of war, was mad with battle frenzy, stripping the armor off those he had slain, when he saw Diomedes. He moved toward the Greek and threw a spear at him, but Athena brushed it aside. When Diomedes cast his spear, she guided it toward Ares. The spear caught the god in the belly. Diomedes pulled his spear back out while Ares shrieked in pain.

The otherwordly sound brought the battle to a halt. Warriors from both sides watched as a black whirl-wind carried the god of war up to Olympus. Hera and Athena returned to Olympus, too, having eliminated the god of war from the field. The battle was left to the mortals.

And so the war continued for yet another long year. Much had yet to happen before the walls of Troy would be breached.

ANCIENT GREECE

RIGHT: Two Greek girls play knucklebones, the gestures of more than two thousand years ago captured in terra cotta. These two figurines, made in fourth-century Greece, were found in southern Italy.

THE AMAZONS

The Amazons are different from the great warrior goddesses of the ancient world. In tales of the goddesses, readers can see remnants of a goddess religion, which is not at ease with the new patriarchal religions. For example, Isis and Hera battle the male gods who replace them.

The tales of the Amazons, creations of the Greeks, grew out of the nature of the Athenian world itself. Athenian society was highly competitive. Men married outside their clan, and while this was supposedly done to consolidate relationships with rival houses, in reality, it brought the daughters of a family's competitors into the family's home, thus bringing the enemy within. As a result, men, and the culture they defined, viewed women with a suspicion tinged with ancient taboos. Necessary for reproduction, women had to be closely supervised or else they could wreak havoc. This theme survives in literature and the visual arts to this day. Images of Amazons in particular can be seen in many museums.

In classical Greek mythology, the Amazons, credited with inventing the cavalry, are valiant foes who must be tamed or vanquished. Like other fantastic animals, Amazon women live on the edge of the familiar universe. Only the bravest, smartest, and wiliest of Greek heroes can overcome an Amazon—and then only through rape or killing. During the Trojan War, however, after Achilles slew

OPPOSITE: This Amazon in Ephesus attends Artemis forever, on a marble frieze from a fourth-century B.C.E. altar to the virgin huntress. Amazons are often depicted with one bare breast; when a female figure has two bare breasts it indicates that she is wounded.

the Amazons' beautiful queen, Penthesilea, he grieved passionately.

Heinrich Schliemann, the nineteenth-century discoverer of Troy, found a terra-cotta shield dating to the late eighth or early seventh century B.C.E. at Tiryns, Greece, showing an Amazon with either Herakles or Theseus. Amazons became fashionable in art depicting Herakles' labors around 575 B.C.E., while in 417 B.C.E. Euripides was the first writer to refer to the Amazon myth, creating a tradition that remained vibrant for centuries, exemplified by the following stories of these fearless women.

QUEEN MYRINE AND THE AMAZONS' EARLY VICTORIES

The ancient sources say the first Amazons came from Libya. There were others, later, from near the Thermodon River, on the Black Sea in today's northern Turkey. The Libyan Amazons disappeared from the earth many generations before the Trojan War. It was the Amazons from the Thermodon who fought at Troy.

The Amazons of Libya were well versed in warfare and lived quite differently from the women of Greece. While the Amazons were engaged in training for battle and serving in the army, the men remained at home and

tended the hearths. Women who served in the army remained virgins until their required military service was completed; then they produced children whom they gave to their husbands for rearing. Girls had their breasts seared as infants so that they might be better able to wield their weapons when they grew older.

The Libyan Amazons lived on an island west of the mythical land of Hespera, which lay in the marsh near a river called Triton. The island, near the edge of the world, was fertile and lush and filled with fruit trees. The women had great herds of goats and sheep. The Amazon people lived well without working hard. They ate fruit from the trees, meat from their herds, and milk from their goats. They didn't eat grain because they didn't practice farming.

The Amazons conquered all the cities on the island, as well as neighboring Libyan cities and nomadic peoples in the area. To celebrate their great victories, the Amazons raised a new city, which they called Peninsula.

Success in battle inspired in the Amazons a desire for more conquest. The Amazon queen, Myrine, raised a great army of thirty thousand foot soldiers and three thousand cavalry. Myrine watched from high ground as her army marched before her. Their shields, which were made of snake skins, glistened in the sunlight. The sound of the women beating their shields with the broadsides of their swords was like thunder. Other women carried lances or bows and arrows.

"Today we will begin the conquest of Atlantis," Myrine said to her lieutenants. "When we take their

city, Cerne, we will make an example of it. Others, seeing the ruins of this city, will want to spare themselves and so will assign their allegiance to us."

Myrine mounted her horse and commanded the archers to attack. The hundreds of arrows taking flight made a sound like a cloud of angry bees. The screams heard from Cerne told of their accuracy. The troops advanced and threw their spears. The defenders fell back. The cavalry charged. The defenders, hopelessly routed, turned and ran.

The Amazon swordswomen brought up the rear. With the defenders in disarray, it was not difficult to follow them into the walled city of Cerne. It didn't take long to subdue the city, and the captives were brought before Myrine.

ABOVE: A Greek pursues a wounded Amazon. The episode is a Roman copy of an artistic quote borrowed from the shield carried by a statue of Athena Parthenos ("The Virgin") by the celebrated fifth-century B.C.E. Greek sculptor Pheidias.

"Put to death any boy of an age to take arms and all the men," commanded Myrine. "Take the women and children as slaves." There were shrieks and much weeping as Myrine's troops carried out her commands.

"Burn it," said Myrine of Cerne. "Burn the city to the ground."

It was done. The flames lit the night sky as the city burned to the ground. Word of what the Amazons had done at Cerne filled all of Atlantis, so that in the following days, representatives from all the cities of the land came before Myrine to offer their friendship and place their cities under her rule.

Myrine received them all and treated them well. To commemorate the event, Myrine raised a new city on the ruins of Cerne, which she named for herself.

In the meeting hall, the newly defeated Atlantians toasted their new mistress.

"We welcome you to Atlantis," said one.

"Yes, indeed," said another, "for with your strong army you can protect us."

"Protect you from what?" said Myrine. "Surely, we have been your greatest enemy."

"Your army of women is indeed formidable," said the first Atlantian. "Perhaps it is stronger and better than that of our enemy, but of this I am not certain."

"Tell me of your enemy," said Myrine. "Who can possibly have an army as good as mine?"

"Yours is not the only army of women. Perhaps it's not even the best," said the second. "The Gorgons, our ancient enemies, are formidable."

"Show me these women warriors who are suppos-edly better than my army," said Myrine.

"The Gorgons are found just beyond the border of Atlantis," said the first. "They come across the border and attack, then pull back."

"I am now the queen of all Atlantis," said Myrine. "I will see to it that you, as my subjects, are protected from these Gorgons."

Myrine led her valiant troops to the border of Atlantis, intending to invade the land of the Gorgons to root out the problem at its source. The Gorgons had seen the approach of the Amazon army, however, and had marshaled their own troops at the border.

Although the fighting was intense, Myrine's troops fought harder and overcame the Gorgons. When the battle was over, the Amazons had taken three thousand prisoners. The rest of the Gorgons fled to the forests for safety.

"Burn the forest," said Myrine. "We shall destroy the Gorgons utterly."

Her troops tried to burn the woods, but the flames were hampered by the winds and the marshy land. The trees at the outside edge were singed, but the fire didn't spread.

"If fate will not allow it," said Myrine to her lieu-tenants, "we shall accept it."

She led her victorious army back to the border of Atlantis. Cooking fires were kindled and soon the smell of roasting meat filled the air. Well fed and drunken with self-congratulation, the Amazons slept. During the night, the captive Gorgons overpowered their guards and attacked their sleeping enemies. Shouts aroused the camp, and the Amazons grabbed their swords and shields and fought back. The Amazons surrounded the Gorgons and killed them all.

The next day, Myrine commanded that the bodies of her fallen comrades be placed on three funeral pyres. Smoke and the smell of burning flesh filled the air. When the flames had subsided, Myrine commanded that the ash mounds be covered with earth.

After her victory, Myrine led her army to Egypt, where she met with Isis' son Horus and signed a treaty with him. Then she and her army rode north and passed on from Egypt, conquering Arabians and Syrians as they went. The Cilecians (in what is now southern Turkey, along the Mediterranean), hearing of her advance, met her, offered her gifts of tribute, and accept-ed her sovereignty. She conquered the people of Taurus (in the mountainous area bordering the Mediterranean and modern Turkey) and Phrygia (in what is today

THE AMAZONS

northern Turkey), and built cities in the countries she conquered. One city she named for herself; others she named for her lieutenants Cyme, Pitane, and Priene. When she conquered the Aegean island of Lesbos, she built a city that she named for her sister, Mitylene. She subdued other islands in the Mediterranean Sea as well.

While Myrine and her army were at sea, a great storm arose. The sky grew black, and the clouds were so low they seemed to sit upon the water. Huge waves washed up over the wooden decks of her ship.

"Save me, Great Mother," Myrine prayed. "Save me from the sea, mother of the gods."

Cybele, the mother of the gods, heard her prayers and led Myrine's ship to Samothrace, an uninhabited island. The soldiers ran the ship aground on a sandy beach, where Myrine offered up a prayer of thanksgiving.

"This island will be dedicated to the Great Mother," Myrine told her lieutenants. "We will not claim this place, for this is the place to which the great goddess has brought us."

So it was that the island of Samothrace became a place of sanctuary, sacred to the goddess Cybele.

Rumors flew about the lands and islands of the eastern Mediterranean that the Amazon queen and her troops had

drowned in the great storm. Mopsus, an outcast from Thrace, raised an army and attacked the lands of the Amazons. He was joined by others, who, like him, were outcasts from their native countries.

Myrine rallied her army and sailed to meet the invaders, planning to surprise the upstarts. The battle raged for days, but the men, coming fresh to battle, had more strength. Myrine's troops were battle-weary after months of campaigning.

Myrine and the greater number of her soldiers were killed in battle. The Amazons who survived continued to fight as they withdrew to the borders of Libya.

OPPOSITE: A Roman gold necklace sports a head of the monster Medusa, the most celebrated of three Gorgon sisters. BELOW: The fearsome Cybele was originally the great Anatolian mother goddess. Like Demeter-Ceres she was a divinity of crops, and her cult was celebrated with orgiastic, sometimes violent rites.

EX·DONO·DVCIS·SFORTIAE·SFORTIA

THE AMAZONS

RIGHT: Roman ruins at Cyrene in what is today Libya. Some of the ancient tales identify this part of the world as the original homeland of the Amazons, whence the armed women rode north and east to conquer lands across the Mediterranean world. The grandeur of the Roman Empire has faded, but fascination with these mythic warriors endures.

HERAKLES AND HIPPOLYTA

Hera harbored ill will against Herakles, a child of faithless Zeus, conceived by guile with his own granddaughter. Though the goddess had suckled him as an infant, she still nursed vengeance in her heart, biding her time.

Herakles grew in strength and fame. His earthly father, Amphitryon, was banished from Tiryns for accidentally killing his uncle, so the family moved north, to Thebes. Herakles adopted the new city as his own, and in time freed the city from the power of evil overlords, the Minyans. Because of his prowess in battle and his fearlessness in facing the enemy, Herakles was given Megara, the daughter of the king of Thebes, in marriage. He loved her dearly, and they lived happily together and had three sons.

That was when Hera struck.

She sent a fit of madness upon Herakles. He went berserk, killing his sons and then his wife when she tried to save the youngest child. After the evil was done, Herakles' madness was taken away. When he saw what he had done, he was overwhelmed with remorse. Amphitryon, who had witnessed what Herakles had done, knew that Hera had stricken him with madness. The father told the son to forgive himself, but Herakles couldn't let himself be absolved.

He traveled to Delphi, where the great oracle told him that to be cleansed of his blood guilt he had to perform twelve labors. The labors would be determined by King Eurystheus, the man who had banished his family from Tiryns. Herakles accepted the punishment willingly, hoping to atone for his bloody crime. That is how Herakles came to steal the girdle of the Amazon queen Hippolyta.

He traveled north from Greece, toward the Pontus, for it was there that the Amazons lived, near the mouth of the Thermodon River, at the city called Themiscyra. Hippolyta, hearing of the Amazons' renowned visitor, met him at his camp.

"What brings you to the kingdom of the Amazons, noble warrior?" asked Hippolyta, admiring his muscular shoulders.

Herakles' Greek warriors stood in rows behind him. Hippolyta's women warriors stood behind her.

"I come on a mission from King Eurystheus," said Herakles. "He asks that I secure from you the magic girdle that you wear."

"Pardon the way my warriors look at you, great warrior. It is your attire. We have never seen a man who wears a lionskin cloak. It is not the custom of these parts." Hippolyta said. "How did you come by your cloak?"

"I killed the lion with my bare hands," said Herakles.

"Really?" said Hippolyta. "That is no mean feat. But what does a man who can strangle lions with his bare hands want with a woman's girdle?"

"I need it to cleanse myself of a crime," said Herakles.

OPPOSITE: This frieze depicts Herakles—who can be identified by his lion skin—attempting to win the girdle, or belt, of Hippolyta, a great Amazon queen.

"A crime?" asked Hippolyta.

"I have been to the oracle of Delphi, who has instructed me to perform the labors that the king demands so that I might purify myself," Herakles told the Amazon.

"The great god Apollo himself speaks through the oracle of Delphi," said Hippolyta piously, "and his priestess must be obeyed."

"Perhaps I could offer you some service in exchange for the girdle," said Herakles.

"Perhaps," said Hippolyta. "I shall think about this. Maybe we could arrive at a mutually agreed upon exchange."

Hippolyta left him then and returned with her women warriors to her city.

Hera had watched the exchange and was not pleased with the result. She had not forgotten her old enmity. She could not directly attack Zeus for his infidelities, but she could work against the children he sired with mortal women. So it was that Hera dis-

BELOW: Amazons are often depicted fighting on horseback with short swords, as on this relief from a fourth-century B.C.E. sarcophagus. OPPOSITE: Herakles battles an Amazon. Although the Amazons lived outdoors, as men did, the artist maintained the convention of giving them fair skin.

THE AMAZONS

guised herself as one of the women warriors and started rumors.

"Did you hear what the Greek men with that giant warrior said?" she asked the woman closest to her.

"What did they say?"

"They said they were prepared to take the girdle by force if Hippolyta doesn't give it willingly," said Hera.

"Really? And how do they propose to do that?" asked the woman.

"They said that an army of women would be easy to defeat," said the disguised goddess.

"Really," said the woman.

Hera left then, to watch the fun from higher up. She watched the rumor fly like wind through the ranks, until it reached the very chambers of the queen.

"Take it by force, will he?" Hippolyta said. "We shall see if an army of women warriors is so easy to defeat."

Hippolyta took the field the following morning, the most valiant of the Amazon warriors beside her. The women warriors were arrayed in battle-ready ranks behind them.

"You are challenged to try to take the girdle," said Hippolyta.

"If that is what you wish," said Herakles.

Aella, a warrior noted for her swiftness, was the first to step forward and to challenge Herakles to personal combat. Aella fought hard, thrusting quickly and pulling back. But Herakles, who was agile for a big man, killed her. Next, the Amazon Philippis stepped forward to take up the challenge. Herakles killed her with his first blow. Prothoe, who had killed seven men before Herakles, then stepped forward. He

killed her as well. The entire honor guard of Hippolyta died on the field that day.

Herakles took Hippolyta prisoner. His men were then loosed on the Amazon army, which had broken and fled when Hippolyta was captured. Nearly the entire Amazon army was destroyed that day. Herakles took one other prisoner—Antiope.

"Queen Hippolyta, I will give you your freedom in exchange for your girdle," said Herakles. "I told you we could reach a mutually beneficial exchange."

"I will give you the girdle," said Hippolyta, "if you will free Antiope."

"You are in no position to bargain," said Herakles. "I will take the girdle. Antiope will be given as a prize to my friend Theseus." Herakles took the girdle and his prisoners and returned to Greece.

HOW THE AMAZONS CAME TO BE BEYOND THE TANAIS

After the battle with the Amazons at the Thermodon River, the Greeks took their prisoners and sailed for home on three ships. After a day at sea, the men slept, but the women warriors didn't. The men hadn't tied them up, telling themselves, "We are at sea. They no longer have weapons. And they are, after all, mere women."

Only the men who steered and the rowers were awake. The women waited until just before moonrise. The only sounds were the creak of wooden oars and the rhythmic slapping of the water. The faint sound of voices, a steersman talking to a companion, came across the water. The women didn't need to speak, moving as people who have trained together do.

Silently the women crept through the boats. On each boat, they crept toward the men who steered. Suddenly, at the same instant, the women sprang upon the steersmen, strangling them and seizing their weapons. Now, the armed women turned on their captors, making their way quietly through the boats, slitting the throats of the men as they slept. Only the sighs of dying men were heard. One man awoke and gave the alarm, but it was too late. Armed and not, the women, with a single loud cry, attacked the remaining men.

As the sun, rosy and new, appeared above the waters, the women threw the bodies of the men overboard and then cleaned the blood from the wooden decks.

The women shouted to one another across the water.

"How do we drive these wooden birds?" called one.

"We can't," answered another. "We must trust in the goddess to bring us safely to land."

So it was that the women let the wind and waves take them to land, trusting that the goddess would steer them to safe harbor. After several days, the ships were washed ashore near Lake Maeotis, in the country of the nomadic Scythians, north of the Black Sea. The women left the boats and waded toward the beach.

"Where are we?" asked one. "How shall we fare here?"

"The goddess will provide," answered another. "After all, she brought us this far."

The highest-ranking woman spoke then. "She will certainly provide. But in the meantime, let's see what's what. Fall in. We will get the lay of the land."

The Amazons fell in line and began their march into the interior of the country. Before long they came upon a herd of horses. Used to working with horses, they walked slowly toward the herd, pausing when the horses stopped grazing to look at them. The women eased toward the horses, and, when each was an arm's length from a horse, in unison, she grabbed its mane and swung her legs over the horse's back. The startled horses reared, but the women were commanding riders and soon tamed them.

"We have weapons, and we have mounts," said the woman in command. "We have everything we need to take what we need."

THE AMAZONS

The Amazons then went in search of human habitation to find food and clothing. They plundered the Scythian countryside, leaving the Scythians in terrified awe of these strange beings. At first, they thought an army of boy soldiers from some foreign land had descended upon them, for none of the warriors sported beards, and the Scythians recognized neither the dress, nor the language of the ruthless invaders.

The Scythians launched attacks against the invading Amazons, killing some of them in the ensuing battles. It was only then that they realized that the warriors they faced were women. This confounded the Scythians. They called a council to discuss how to deal with the problem.

"It is against the natural order of things to take arms against women," said one man.

"I agree. It is not wise to kill women in battle," said another. "But how can we protect ourselves?"

"Perhaps we should send our young men, men filled with vigor, out to meet these maidens," said the first. "It would be to our advantage to have children from so valiant a race, would it not?"

"Ah," said the second. "I see. But what if the women fight?"

"The young men will be given orders not to engage the women in combat," said a third.

"Yes, yes," said the first. "That would do it. Get the women used to the young men, much like taming a wild horse."

So the old men sent out an army of young men, equal in number to the Amazons. The young men were given orders not to engage the women in combat, but to set up camp nearby and to follow the women in all that

OPPOSITE: This fleeing maiden from the Sacred House in Eleusis, Greece, her long skirts roiling in her distress, is the historical reality that belied the legends of the Amazons. ABOVE: An archaic-period young woman gazes into another world.

they did. If the Amazons came against them in battle, the young men were ordered to pull back. When the women stopped and camped, the men were to stop and camp.

The young men obeyed their orders, and after a few weeks, the camps of the young men and the warrior maidens were quite close together. Both camps spent the days practicing the arts of war, taking care of their weapons, and performing feats on horseback.

The young men noticed that at noon each day, the Amazons scattered in ones and twos, going off to bathe. One day a Scythian youth followed one of the Amazons to where she bathed. She made motions for him to follow her into the water, which he did. After they bathed, they made love on the bank of the river. The Amazon, through sign language, agreed to meet the young man the next day. She told him to bring a friend, and she agreed to bring a friend.

Word spread among the troops, and the trysts multiplied. Soon the two camps joined together, and each Amazon took a mate. The men were

unable to learn the language of the women, but the women, being very adept, learned the language of the Scythians. They lived together in the countryside for some time.

One day, one of the young Scythians addressed the Amazons. "We don't need to live such a rustic life," he pointed out. "All of us," and he gestured toward the other young men, "come from wealthy families. We have parents and goods. If you will give up this lifestyle, we can live in peace and prosperity among our people."

The leader of the Amazons spoke then. "We could never fit in with your womenfolk," she said. "Look at us. We know the skills of war, not of cloth weaving or other womanly arts."

The Amazon women murmured agreement.

"If you wish to remain with us as our husbands, we will agree to be

THE AMAZONS

THESEUS AND ANTIOPE

There is disagreement about whether Herakles gave Antiope to Theseus, or whether Theseus went to the land near the Thermodon and captured the Amazon himself at a later time. Also, some say it was Hippolyta that Theseus captured, for he and the Amazon he took had a son named Hippolytus. However it happened, Theseus took the captive Amazon warrior to Athens.

Herakles and his men had returned to Greece. The Amazons had valiantly overcome their captors and sailed to the land of the Scythians, where they married the young men and created a new people beyond the Tanais River. Their alliances with the Scythian men created bonds with the ruling houses of Scythia, and so it was that the Scythians allied themselves with the Amazons in their onslaught against Athens.

"Shall we let this affront go, like poor-spirited weaklings?" asked the highest-ranking Amazon regarding Antiope's capture. "Or shall we defend our honor and retrieve Antiope from the enemy?"

The Amazons voted unanimously to fight for their honor. The young Scythian men they had married acquiesced, as they tended to do. The new Amazon army crossed the Strait of Kertch, near the Black Sea, and marched down through Thrace until they reached the land of the Greeks and the city of Athens.

your mates, but you must go to your parents and ask for your inheritance and then return to us here."

The young men discussed the proposition among themselves. They agreed that it was a sound plan. The young men went back to their parents' homes, asked for their inheritances, then returned to their soldier-lovers.

"We must leave this land," said the Amazon leader. "Your parents will resent us because we have taken you from them, and we have stolen from the Scythians throughout the area."

The young men agreed to follow the Amazons. The new tribe moved their camp to the land beyond the Tanais River, today the Don, where they became known as the Sauromatae.

ABOVE: This head of Athena from the Parthian Monument in Ephesus seems to be issuing a divine, timeless call.
OPPOSITE: The Battle of Troy is one of the most enduring themes in European art. Here, a Greek and a Trojan warrior meet on the field.

The Amazons fought hard and bravely. They commanded the countryside surrounding Athens and began taking over the streets of the city, one by one. Finally, they pitched their camp inside the city itself. They held all of downtown Athens.

Theseus, with Antiope, came to meet the invaders. Antiope now fought for her husband, the father of her son. Theseus and his troops quartered themselves near the Amazons. At first neither side moved to attack, until at last, Theseus charged the Amazon troops. The Amazons hit back hard.

The Greeks fell back from the city's main gate, all the way to the shrine of the Eumenides. But the Amazons' right flank crumpled near the Palladium, the precinct of Athens sacred to Athena. As the Amazons fell back from the Lyceum, the Greek troops engaged them in hand-to-hand combat, killing many as they drove the warriors back into their encampment. For three months, fierce battles raged from neighborhood to neighborhood.

Antiope went to propose a truce to her former companions. "Will you make peace?" she asked.

"Why do you, the one defiled by these Greeks, come to speak to us of peace?" asked Molpadia, the leader of the Amazons. "Why don't you join us in the attack?"

"I have a son," said Antiope. "I can't abandon him."

"Leave him to his father's people," said Molpadia. "You are one of us."

"I can't."

"We will not make peace with these Greeks," said Molpadia.

Antiope returned to Theseus and gave him the message. The fighting continued. During the battle, unbeknownst to Theseus and the Greeks, Antiope scoured the battlefield, finding wounded Amazons and secretly stealing them away to Chalcis so that they could be healed. Those who

died, she buried there, and a monument called the Amazoneum was erected in their memory.

Some say Antiope then died as a result of a spear thrown by Molpadia as the latter woman stood on the battlefield beside her husband, fighting valiantly. Others say that is false.

At last the fighting came to an end. The Amazons signed a treaty, possibly at Antiope's pleading. In times to come, the Athenians would offer a sacrifice to the Amazons just before the feast of Theseus. The Amazons left Athens and returned to their new Scythian homeland, but images of the Amazons were carved on Athena's temple.

THE DEATH OF PENTHESILEA

Word of the Greeks encamped on the plains of Troy spread throughout the ancient world. Stories of the great battles and heroes reached as far as Thermodon, the land of the Amazons. Penthesilea, the Amazon queen, heard of the great war.

She yearned to go and fight. Her heart was burdened by guilt, for she had killed her beloved sister. Throwing her spear at a speck of brown in the underbrush, thinking it the stag they pursued, she had struck her sister, who was beating the bushes to bring the stag to flight. Goaded by grief, Penthesilea longed to escape the people and places that reminded her of her sorrow.

She determined to go to Troy to cleanse her blood guilt by fighting on the side of the Trojans, and with her went her twelve princesses.

BELOW: The Trojan king, Priam, pleads with Achilles to cede him the body of Hector, Priam's beloved son, for proper burial. OPPOSITE: Achilles impiously dragged Hector's body behind his chariot, below the walls of Troy.

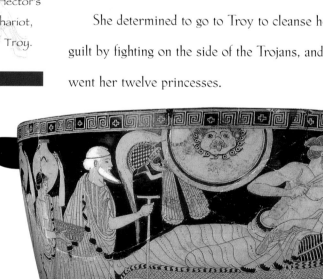

The people of Troy were amazed at these beauties who rode astride like men, wore armor, and carried spears. Although tales of Amazons had been spoken of around campfires, there were those who maintained that women warriors were the stuff of myth.

Priam, king of Troy, burdened with sorrow at the death of his son Hector, came to meet Penthesilea and her women warriors as they rode into the great walled city.

"Welcome, child of Ares," said Priam. "You bring new hope to an old man weighed down with sorrow and loss."

"Do the Greeks press you?" asked Penthesilea.

"The Greek Achilles has killed my son Hector and has arrogantly and impiously dragged his body around the ramparts of Troy, pulling it behind his chariot. To see my beautiful son treated so…" Priam couldn't continue.

"The glorious Hector is dead then," said Penthesilea. "I had hoped to fight at his side. If we can't fight with him, we will fight to avenge his death instead."

Penthesilea dismounted from her horse and removed the golden crested helmet she wore. Murmurs arose from the crowd. Her hair was golden, and her features as noble as the war goddess Athena.

"It is obvious she is the daughter of the war god," said one. "Only one of divine birth could be so lovely."

"Surely Athena herself is less splendid," said another.

Penthesilea, hearing the whispers, was filled with pride at the comparison to Athena. It was foolish to let her heart fill with pride—mortals who dared to compare themselves with Athena usually suffered for their hubris.

"Please, come into the great hall," said Priam. "You and your warrior maids will be feasted."

Priam led Penthesilea and her twelve companions into the great hall, where he bid the women of his house serve them and see to their comforts. Hector's widow, Andromache, oversaw the serving of food and drink.

"If you can avenge the death of my beloved son," said Priam, "I will give you anything that you desire."

"I need no other reward than to take the life of Achilles, who has slain your son and so misused his battle-weary corpse," said Penthesilea.

Andromache spilled the wine that she poured. She moved to mop up the stain, and her movements betrayed her anger.

"Such idle boasts," thought Andromache, "for a woman to think she can slay Achilles when the greatest of warriors, my own Hector, couldn't."

Priam didn't seem to notice. He was too entranced with the lovely visitors. For indeed, all the Amazons were tall and well shaped. Their faces were animated. Their eyes sparkled. They had the look about them of people who spend a good deal of time outside, healthy and full of vigor.

"To your success," said Priam, and he lifted his cup to toast Penthesilea and her Amazons.

They drank and feasted until late. At last, couches were spread with skins for the Amazons in the great hall, close to the hearth. Athena waited until Penthesilea slept, then slipped into the Amazon's dreams. Penthesilea dreamt of her father. He congratulated her for killing Troy's greatest enemy, and her heart swelled with pride for she knew that she would kill Achilles. As dawn approached, Athena retreated to Olympus.

"That will teach the overreaching Amazon to compare herself to me," thought Athena. "Too much confidence is the undoing of many a warrior."

The warrior maids awoke, prepared for battle, and mounted their steeds. Penthesilea rode a prancing thoroughbred, straining to run. The

Amazons' gleaming armor reflected the sun's rays. On their heads they wore golden helmets with crests of golden horsehair. Each carried two javelins, a strong sword, and a shield. Proud Penthesilea laughed for joy.

"To battle, my warriors," she yelled. "I am Ares' child, and we go to take revenge on the Greeks."

The Trojans fell in behind the Amazons and together they took the field. Penthesilea and her maidens led the charge. The Greeks rushed to meet them, and the battle was soon engaged. Achilles, however, was nowhere to be found upon the battlefields, for he had remained behind in camp, mourning a fallen comrade. The Amazons lent new hope to the Trojans, and the battle seemed to go their way. They fought all

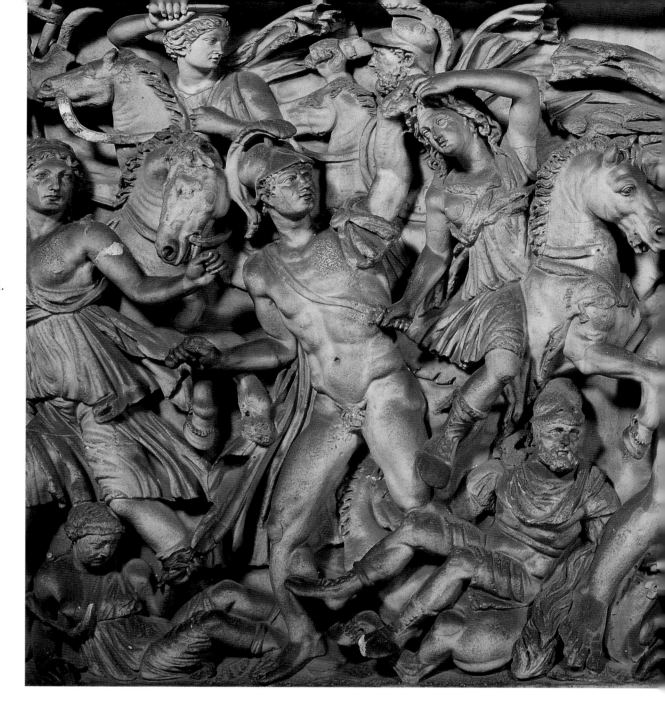

day. But Clonie, who rode beside Penthesilea, was struck by a spear. It caught her below her navel, disemboweling her and throwing her from her horse. She died on the battlefield.

Her death filled Penthesilea with rage. She threw a javelin at the man who had killed Clonie. The spear went through his throwing arm, pinning it to his chest. His friends dragged him from the battlefield, and he died in their arms. Rage filled the Greeks as well. So the battle was renewed with hate. Bremusa was the next Amazon to die, stabbed through the right breast. Evandre and Thermodosa rushed to her side, but both were killed. Derinoe was swept from her horse

when a spear struck her in the throat. Derimacheia was beheaded with one sword stroke. As each fell, Penthesilea was filled with ever greater rage.

Deliberate as a hunting lioness, Penthesilea took vengeance upon the Greeks. Her rage filled them with fear as she killed all within her sword's range. The Greeks began to run, and the Trojans, sensing a rout, fell hard on their heels. The battlefield was red with carnage—speared horses, their lifeblood soaking the field, and corpses of men and Amazons fallen and mangled.

From the ramparts of Troy, the women watched the battle.

ABOVE: Penthesilea,
an Amazon queen,
fought against the Greeks
in the Trojan War. Achilles
slew her in battle, then
fell in love with her lifeless body.

The women with Tisiphone, roused by her words, shouted their agreement. They grabbed weapons and headed for the gates.

But Theano, an older woman, stopped them. "Where do you think you're going?" she demanded. "Do you suppose that you who have done nothing but women's work can hope to be of any help to a woman trained to fight? The reason Penthesilea carries the field is because she has trained for war her entire life. She has carried out the duties of a man. It is foolishness to think you can become warriors in an afternoon."

The younger women listened to her counsel and looked at one another, feeling silly. They returned to their vantage point and watched Penthesilea, at the head of the Trojans, pushing the Greeks back to

"It fills my heart with valor to see such a woman," exclaimed Tisiphone. "Why do we merely stand here and watch helplessly? Why aren't we in the fray? For so long, we have watched our husbands and brothers and sons and fathers die at the hands of the Greeks. How much more must we endure? It would be better to die nobly on the battlefield, led by such a woman, than to be carried off with our children into slavery by those very men who have taken from us the men that we loved."

their ships. Then there was a quickening among the Greek troops, for Achilles now joined the battle. He was joined by his comrade Aias. The Greek troops stopped their retreat and turned to face the Amazon-led Trojans.

"At last," shouted Penthesilea, "the noble Achilles deigns to come to the battlefield. Now will I have my vengeance."

She drove her horse directly toward the two Greek heroes. Achilles and Aias stood shoulder to shoulder,

THE AMAZONS

their shields touching, facing her onslaught. Penthesilea let fly a spear at Aias, but the shaft bounced off his shield, splitting into fragments. She threw her second spear, but it bounced off Aias' greave.

"Are you afraid to do battle with me?" demanded Penthesilea. "You take refuge behind your shields, the two of you. But I am not afraid of the odds. Let me show you the strength of an Amazon heart. I am your equal. I can take you both. I am the daughter of the god of war himself."

Aias laughed. "I leave her to you, Achilles." Aias led a charge against the Trojan troops.

"So you think you can achieve what even Hector could not?" said Achilles. "You have no discretion.

Not even the war god can save you from your folly. You are not the only hero on the field with divine blood in your veins."

Achilles threw his mighty battle spear at Penthesilea. It caught her above the right breast, driving deep into her flesh. Scarlet stained her golden armor, and she gasped for breath. Achilles ran to pull the Amazon from her horse.

As Penthesilea struggled to draw her sword, Achilles drove his second spear into her horse. The spear went through the horse, wounding Penthesilea, and both the Amazon queen and the horse fell. The Trojans, seeing her pinned to the earth by her fallen horse, turned and ran for the ramparts of Troy.

"That didn't take much," said Achilles, laughing. "What a foolhardy woman to take on a manly task."

Penthesilea and her horse labored for breath, then both died. Achilles bent over to take the spoils of war, pulling the helmet from Penthesilea's head. He groaned.

"What a beautiful, beautiful woman," he said. "What a waste this was. I would much rather have taken her home to bed than to leave her like this."

"A fine wife she would have made!" teased Thersites. "How would you have shown a woman adept at war how to weave and spin?"

THE AMAZONS

"Still this is a great pity," mused Achilles. "To waste so much beauty…"

"Maybe you would have been better off if she had pierced your heart with the ashen variety of spear," teased Thersites.

Achilles punched Thersites beneath the ear, and he fell to the ground, dead. Then Thersites' brother turned on Achilles, and the Greeks had to separate the two.

"Enough. Enough. You need cooler heads," one said. But it was too late.

The Greeks began to fight among themselves.

Recalling ancient quarrels, the Greeks soon turned the battlefield into a heated free-for-all, which was finally interrupted by messengers from King Priam.

"I ask a boon," said one of the messengers. "My lord, Priam, asks that you release the body of the Amazon queen Penthesilea so that she may be buried with honor, as her rank and valor deserve. He asks also that we have time to bury our dead."

"This is bold," said a Greek. "Achilles merits the Amazon's goods."

"The spoils from Penthesilea are mine to give," said Achilles. "I agree."

He let the Trojan messengers take the body of Penthesilea back to Troy, her armor intact. Priam placed her body on a huge funeral pyre, and Trojans brought gifts to put on the fire. So Penthesilea was honored for her courage and great heart. The flame was doused with wine; her ashes were gathered and placed in a casket, which was buried beside her fallen Amazon warriors on the fateful plain of Troy.

THE ROMAN WORLD

The Italian peninsula has been inhabited since earliest times, as cave paintings in the northeast attest. There were many tribes and peoples, speaking several languages and worshiping all kinds of deities, from local gods of springs and other natural sites to sophisticated divinities such as those of the wealthy, literate Etruscans—famous for their fortune-telling—in the north.

Greek colonists arrived in southern Italy and the island of Sicily in around the eighth century B.C.E., bringing with them their ancient pantheon, which, through their commercial influence, soon became widespread throughout Italy. Syncretism, the practice of combining the characteristics of several religions or divinities, was very common in the Mediterranean world, and Italy was no exception. As the Romans conquered their neighbors over the course of the five centuries preceding the Common Era, the victors absorbed many of the beliefs of the vanquished.

The Greek authors found the Etruscans scandalous, for aristocratic Etruscan women ate and socialized not only with their husbands, but also with men who were not their husbands. (Married Greek women were restricted to quarters within their husband's home, and had no public life at all.)

The Romans had deities of their own, but as they came to power they combined the goddesses and gods of the Etruscans, their

OPPOSITE: This illustration, from an early sixteenth-century French manuscript on the lives of famous women, portrays Minerva, the Roman version of Athena. Here, Minerva is not just in armor but dressed like a male soldier. Like her Greek alter ego, she carries a golden staff.

neighbors to the north, and those of the Greeks, to the south. During the formation of the Roman Empire, they would continue to adopt foreign divinities, such as Isis, who would have an important temple and cult in the city of Rome. The Greek goddess Hera became Juno, and Athena became Minerva. Like the Greek divinities, the Romans' shifted qualities. For example, Minerva, like her counterpart, was the goddess of wisdom, and specifically of strategy in war (as opposed to Ares-Mars, the god who inspires blood lust). But unlike the stern virgin Athena, Minerva was sometimes portrayed as a mother.

Artemis became Diana, also a chaste huntress and sister of Apollo, who alone retained his name. The third virgin goddess was Hestia, goddess of the hearth, who became Vesta, with a temple in the Roman forum. There she was served by six priestesses, who tended the flame of the city, which must never go out, upon pain of death.

Aphrodite, the goddess of love, "the foam-risen," became Venus, and in the transformation lost almost all of her power. Originally she was as mighty and terrible as Mars, capable of bestowing serene and faithful love, but also of arousing mad and fateful passions.

Socially, the position of women in Rome, which was never as restricted as in Greece, became further liberalized over time. In later years, they acquired not only names, but certain rights under certain circumstances, such as that of owning property. They

ABOVE: The Roman Minerva represents the combination of an Etruscan goddess and the Greek Athena; their sacred bird is the owl of wisdom.
RIGHT: This mosaic portrait from Pompeii captures the dignity of the ideal Roman matron, the wife and mother of citizens.

tended to command respect as the keepers of the home and the educators of children; Juno, who protected married women, was an honored goddess. Perhaps because Roman society was never quite as sexually polarized as the Greek world, the native myths are not as violent toward women.

Greek culture united a quarreling group of cities, and just as the Greeks had their *Iliad* and *Odyssey*, Rome, under Caesar Augustus, the first Roman emperor, had to have its own epic to legitimize it. The poem was Virgil's *Aeneid*, which tells of the travels of Aeneas, a Trojan prince, and his followers after the fall of Troy.

In Virgil's epic, Carthage, Rome's rival in the eastern Mediterranean, is under the protection of the war-like Juno, who wishes to defeat Venus, mother of Aeneas. Aeneas meets the great queen and founder of the city, Dido, with tragic results. Virgil portrays her as a courageous and noble-hearted person, a wise ruler, and a faithful lover (if a little more passionate than a good Roman woman would be). Nevertheless,

politics and propaganda require her to lose in this duel of the goddesses.

A number of the Roman myths formulated in historical times reveal intentionally propagandistic messages. This is true in the case of Dido and Aeneas, and also in the tale of Camilla. While Dido, a foreign woman, becomes a warrior to take the place of her husband, the Roman Camilla is patriotically trained by her father, for love of their homeland—their beloved Roman hearth.

BELOW: In this painting by the Venetian artist Jacopo Tintoretto, Minerva, in her role as giver and preserver of civilization, shields Peace and Abundance from the onslaught of war-mad Mars.

LEFT: One of the most famous images of ancient Rome, the Coliseum opened to the public in A.D. 79, the year Pompeii erupted. This vast arena was the scene of infamous battles staged for the entertainment of the masses. At least one female gladiator "performed" here: she was a slave, fighting for her freedom.

THE BETRAYAL OF DIDO

Dido's father betrothed her to a young man named Sychaeus. She was greatly pleased, for she loved him with all her heart. Her joy, however, turned to great sorrow and shame, for on the day of the wedding, Sychaeus didn't appear. Dido retreated to her rooms, where she cried herself to sleep. Sychaeus came to her in her dreams.

The sight of him caused Dido to cry out in her sleep, for he was covered in blood.

"My dearest," she whispered, "what has befallen you?"

"Your brother Pygmalion has murdered me," Sychaeus said, "even as you waited for me at the altar."

"But why?" Dido asked. "Why would he strike you and in so doing strike me?"

"He is mad with jealousy," replied Sychaeus. "He desires my wealth for himself. I fear for your safety. Without me to protect you, you are at his mercy. You must flee Tyre this very night."

"But how can I leave my home?" asked Dido. "How will I live in the world, away from my father's house?"

"We are married," said Sychaeus, "even if your brother has sought to divide us. My wealth is yours, dearest."

Sychaeus stooped to whisper into Dido's ear, telling her where to find his great treasure. He kissed her cheek, and she awoke with a start. Dido woke her maidservant and told her what she had seen and heard. Together they crept through the moonless city of Tyre, making their way to Sychaeus' land holdings just outside the city. Sychaeus' servants welcomed her and pledged themselves to serve her, for they acknowledged her as their mistress.

Dido directed workmen to dig into the earth where her beloved had told her to, and there they found buried chests filled with exquisite gold and silver. The treasure was loaded onto carts, and Dido and Sychaeus' servants fled toward the harbor, where Sychaeus' ship lay at anchor, ready to sail.

So it was that a woman captained a Tyrian ship. Dido sailed with her ghostly husband's household toward the west, away from her brother's mad greed. They landed on the North African coast, where Juno led them to a place where they found the skull of a horse. Thus did the goddess show them where her city was to be founded.

Dido bought land and the great city Carthage began to rise, as Dido set the men who had come with her to building the walls of the city.

Meanwhile, the Greeks had destroyed the towered city of Troy, leaving few survivors. The Trojan Aeneas, like Dido, fled his homeland with the people of his house and other Trojans in twenty ships. Mighty storms, driven by Juno's unrelenting hatred of the Trojans, pounded Aeneas' vessels. The fleet was dispersed. Venus, fearing for her son Aeneas' safety, flew to father Jupiter and begged him to intervene.

"Father, your wife, Juno, will destroy my son," cried Venus. "You promised that he would father a great race at Rome. Help him or he will be destroyed."

"There is nothing to fear, daughter," said Jupiter. "Your son Aeneas is indeed bound for great things. I will speak to the god of winds to calm the storms."

Jupiter sent his command to the god of winds. Finally, the seas calmed, and Aeneas and his crew sighted the North African coast. They took their seven remaining ships to shore, where they found a quiet cove that was sheltered from the sea's rough weather by a small island. It was a beautiful place, where mountains came down to meet the sea and a white sand beach spread from the seaside to the foot of the mountain. Aspen trees shimmered in the breeze while fresh water cascaded down the mountainside. Someone had carved

seats from the living rock in a grotto. Aeneas and his men gave thanks to the gods, reveling in the feel of warm sand beneath their feet.

Aeneas went in search of game. He hadn't far to go: a herd of deer had come to drink from the fresh water of the grotto. He killed seven deer, one for each of his ships. That night, the weary Trojans feasted and toasted their fallen comrades.

Venus wasn't idle during the night. While Jupiter had taken care of calming the storm, she took it upon herself to see that Aeneas and his men would be well received by Dido and the people of Carthage.

The next morning Aeneas and a companion, Achates, decided to look over the country where they had landed. They thought at first that perhaps the land was not inhabited, for the fields appeared to be uncultivated, but as they traveled on, climbing toward higher ground, they came upon the walls of the city. Many people were working diligently within, building the city. Some workmen laid stone foundations for homes while others dug drainage ditches. The harbor was being dredged. The Tyrians had built a great temple dedicated to Juno in the heart of the city.

Aeneas and Achates looked with wonder, for the carvings upon the temple were exquisite, each panel showing a scene from the Trojan War. As Aeneas and Achates looked on, the streets filled with fanfare and a great procession approached. Dido herself came to the temple. She took her seat upon the throne beneath Juno's gate.

"Friend," asked Aeneas of a bystander who stood watching the ceremony, "who is the great lady who sits upon the throne of Carthage?"

"That is our queen, Dido," answered the Tyrian.

"Why does she come to the temple?" asked Aeneas.

"She comes to hear petitions," answered the man. "If anyone is in need, they have only to ask."

As Aeneas watched, men of his company, men he had feared lost at sea, made their way to Dido and knelt before her. He motioned to Achates, and they moved closer to the front.

"Great queen," said Ilioneus, "take pity on us Trojans. We have been driven from our homes and forced to flee across inhospitable seas."

"What do you need from me?" asked Dido.

"We ask that you protect our ships, gracious queen," answered Ilioneus. "We mean no one any harm. We are on our way to Italy. We don't intend to stop here very long. We have been driven to your shores by unkind fate, and while here we have been met by suspicion and threats. I promise that if you help us to repair our ships, King Acestes of Sicily, himself a Trojan, will reward you for your kindness."

"I apologize if you have been treated harshly," said Dido. "Surely, you men of Troy must understand our caution. We are a new city in a new land. It would be foolhardy not to have sentries on all borders. But, indeed, I have heard of the mighty deeds of the men of Troy. You are welcome here.

"Perhaps your leader, Aeneas, has himself been driven to land. I will send out messengers to scour the countryside for him."

At the kind words of Dido, Aeneas and Achates came forward from the crowd and made themselves known. Their fellow Trojans greeted them with open arms and tears. Dido watched as Aeneas greeted all. She found him very attractive.

"Thank you for your kindness," said Aeneas, turning to her and kneeling before her.

"You are most welcome, man of Troy," said Dido.

"May I ask, queen, how it is that you came to know of the Trojans?"

"Many refugees sought out my father in the cities of Tyre and Sidon, seeking to make their homes there. Even the enemies of Troy spoke admiringly of your noble people. I used to sit, enraptured by their stories. You are very welcome in my home, Aeneas."

"Thank you, great queen," said Aeneas. "With your permission, I will send a messenger to my ships to let my son know that I am safe, and to ask him to join us."

"Of course," said Dido.

Aeneas sent word to his son to bring the few treasures they had salvaged from burning Troy. Dido sent cattle, swine, ewes, and lambs to the ships and ordered her household to prepare a feast.

Venus watched closely, hidden from human sight by a divine mist; she didn't trust the Tyrian queen. She sped to her son, Cupid, and together they plotted to abduct Aeneas' son. Cupid would take his place. It would be his job to fill Dido with passion for Aeneas.

So it was that Cupid took the form of Iulus, Aeneas' son, and sat close by Dido that night at the feasting. They ate well and drank good wine in the house of Dido. Musicians filled the night with song. The memory of

Sychaeus faded a bit for Dido as she watched Aeneas with his men. She engaged the Trojan hero in conversation, begging him to tell her of the men who fought at Troy. Sleep finally overcame them, and the Trojans made their way to their quarters. Dido went to her own bed-chamber, but sleep eluded her.

Dawn came and found her still awake. Finally, Dido arose, bathed her face, dressed, and went in search of her sister, Anna.

"You're up early," said Anna.

"I can't sleep. Too much excitement, perhaps," said Dido.

"Excitement, is it?" said Anna, laughing.

"What do you mean?" asked Dido.

ABOVE: By the Renaissance, the ancient goddesses had lost all their mythic powers. In Sandro Botticelli's fresco, Venus, formerly the embodiment of the creative principle of life, is a discreet, dignified, and aristocratic lady. OPPOSITE: Venus' popularity grew with the political rise of Julius Caesar, whose family traced its lineage to her.

"I saw you two last night. You were bending low to whisper into the Trojan's ear," Anna teased.

"I wasn't whispering into his ear," said Dido. "It was difficult to hear one another with the noise of the feast. I was trying to be a good hostess, asking him of his troubles."

"Ah, troubles," said Anna. "So, a man's troubles have kept you awake."

"He has been so misused by fate," said Dido. "The years of endless war have taken their toll."

"So, you like Aeneas, then?" asked Anna. She laughed as Dido's cheeks flushed.

"I must confess," said Dido, "if I hadn't forsworn marriage, I might be tempted."

"You are too young to forswear marriage, Dido," said Anna softly.

At that Dido burst into tears. "I am being untrue to Sychaeus. I gave him all my love. This is foolhardy."

"Dido, my sister," said Anna, "you are young. Do you mean never to have children? Never to know the joys of love again?"

"I never knew such loss as when Sychaeus died," cried Dido. "I can't face such a loss again."

"If you won't marry for love," said Anna, "think about your people and where we are. Marry for strength. We are surrounded by enemies on every side. It would be well for us if you married a man who knows about war. And you would not find Aeneas unpleasing."

Dido went to the temple and poured libations to Juno between the horns of a white heifer. She searched for omens. She walked the streets of the city, but didn't notice the progress of the workmen. At last she made her way to her house and invited Aeneas to travel the city with her. She described her plans for the city. That night, the feast continued. She asked Aeneas to tell his story yet again. The feast ended and the guests went home. Dawn found Dido again awake. Days went by in this fashion. Without Dido's close supervision, the building in Carthage stopped.

Juno saw and was alarmed. She knew that Venus had had a hand in Dido's loss of interest.

"You and your son have done good work," said Juno. "It has taken two gods to outwit one human woman. Good work, indeed."

Venus ignored her.

"I have a proposal," said Juno. "I'm not against Dido loving your son Aeneas, but why not have them marry so that the houses of Troy and Tyre become strong?"

Venus pretended to listen, but she knew Juno was up to something, because Juno was against any Trojan ruling an Italian kingdom.

"Do as you wish," said Venus. "I will not hinder you."

The next day Dido asked Aeneas to go hunting. As they pursued the game, Juno brought up a wild storm, filled with thunder and hail. The hunters scattered, searching for shelter. Dido and Aeneas took refuge in the same cave. They sat close together for warmth, and soon found themselves in each other's arms. They spent the night in the cave, rejoining their companions the next day when the sun filled the sky. From that day on, Dido and Aeneas spent many hours together.

Rumors flew throughout the kingdom. Prayers of complaint rose to Jupiter. Aeneas' rivals bitterly denounced the Trojan to Jupiter. Finally, Zeus intervened. He sent Mercury, the messenger of the gods, to command Aeneas to continue his journey to Italy. The god appeared to Aeneas, filling him with fear. Mercury told Aeneas to leave Carthage quickly and without fuss.

Aeneas did as he was commanded. He prepared his fleet to set sail, but said nothing to Dido. Dido, however, noticed his changed mood.

"You're leaving me then," said Dido. "You, the hero of a dreadful war, couldn't tell me this to my face? My love means nothing to you?"

"I have laid no claim to you as husband," said Aeneas.

"You dishonor me among my people and the peoples who surround us," said Dido.

"I can't stay," said Aeneas. "How can you, who have created a city, deny the Trojans a land of their own? I must provide for my son. The god commands me to go."

"So this is what I get for taking in a beggar," said Dido. "I will not keep you here if you will not stay. Get out."

Aeneas left, ordered his ships loaded, and prepared to put out to sea.

Dido called her sister, Anna, to her.

"Anna, go to Aeneas. Tell him I am sorry for the ugly words I spoke. Tell him I don't ask for marriage. Tell him I only ask that he stay through the winter, until the weather is calmer."

Anna ran to Aeneas, but he would not be swayed. Anna returned.

"So be it," said Dido quietly. "Do me one last kindness, sister."

"Anything," said Anna.

"I have spoken to the priestess. She has told me that to be free of this man, I must destroy everything

that reminds me of him. Therefore, see to it that a funeral pyre is erected in the courtyard. Bring from the house every-thing that was his and lay it on the pyre. Bring out the marriage bed as well."

"I will do so," said Anna.

Dido could not let her sister see the depth of her loss. Cupid's arrows had wounded her very soul, but love was not her destiny.

At dawn, Dido sent Sychaeus' old nurse for Anna. Dido commanded them to deck themselves for a sacrifice. She went then to the funeral pyre and mount-ed it. She sat on her marriage bed, clasp-ing Aeneas' sword. She cursed him, then fell on the sword.

The servant woman in the courtyard saw the blood and raised a shout. Anna and the old nurse came running. Dido yet lived.

"Sister, why did you lie to me?" Anna asked. "Why not tell me the truth so that I could have joined you? You have condemned us all."

Juno took pity at last, and life fled Dido. Anna and the old nurse lit the funeral pyre. Its blaze climbed so high that the Trojans could see it from the decks of their ships.

RIGHT: This frieze is a Roman copy of a fifth-century B.C.E. original by Kallimachos. The women are maenads, also called bacchantes, who dance in honor of Dionysus, the god of wine. Their swirling robes express their sacred intoxication. According to legend, at the height of their ritual madness the maenads, whose name comes from the Greek word for "being insane," would capture wild beasts, tear them apart, and eat the flesh raw.

CAMILLA

Camilla was a favorite of the goddess Diana. Her father, Metabus, had been an unjust king of the Volscians. His subjects rebelled and drove him from the city of Privernum (the present-day city of Priverno, in central Italy). The only companion he took as he fled was his baby daughter, Camilla, who had been named for her late mother. His rebellious subjects chased him to the banks of the river Amasenus, which was swollen with floodwaters.

Metabus tied the infant Camilla to his oak spear, and, praying to Diana, threw the spear across the raging waters. His weapon carried its precious burden to safety on the farthest bank. Pursuers hot behind him, Metabus leapt into the river's current and swam to the opposite shore. It was a desperate act. Those in pursuit

lacked the same ardor and ceased their chase. Thus it was that Camilla was dedicated to Diana.

From that time on, Metabus shunned the companionship of people other than his daughter. He took her into the hills, far from cities and civilization, and, there, amid the shepherds and their flocks, he nursed his infant daughter. When she cried for food, Metabus milked wild mares on the hillside.

When she was just a toddler, her first toy was a javelin. Metabus made a tiny pointed lance, a bow, and a quiver filled with arrows for her. He knew nothing of how to teach a young girl to braid her hair. He didn't provide her with elegant robes, as would befit the daughter of a king. She wore a wild tiger's skin.

As a young girl, Camilla learned to hunt birds, such as cranes and swans. Her father showed her how to use a slingshot, and she became an excellent

ABOVE: In this painting by Rubens, Diana and her nymphs are somehow more naked than the bestial satyrs. Here they are pale indoor women, whereas Roman Diana was a mistress of the wild.
OPPOSITE: Many ancient representations of goddesses retain traces of the mysterious power of the original myths.

markswoman. She grew into a beautiful young woman. Tuscan mothers sought her for a daughter-in-law, but she would have none of their sons. She dedicated herself to Diana, the chaste goddess, savoring her maidenhood and her freedom. She gathered to herself a troop of horsemen, but her closest companions were three Italian women, warriors like herself, named Larina, Tulla, and Tarpeia. Together they would rush boldly into the thick of battles, eager for victory. So when word came that the Trojans threatened Latium, Camilla came with her cavalry to offer her services to Turnus, the country's ruler.

▬▬ THE WAR FOR LATIUM ▬▬

How Turnus had come to rule Latium is in itself a story. Aeneas, fleeing Carthage in search of the lands the gods had promised to him and his progeny, landed his ships in Latium. He sought out the king, Latinus, and asked to buy a small parcel of land. Latinus however, saw the coming of the Trojans as the fulfillment of the gods' will: the oracles had told him that his daughter, Lavinia, must marry a foreigner. Aeneas, it seemed to the king, must be the foreigner whose coming the diviners had foreseen.

"Welcome, stranger," said Latinus. "I have been waiting for you."

"How can this be?" said Aeneas. "I myself didn't know that I was coming to this shore."

"The oracles foretold the coming of a stranger. It is to that stranger that my daughter, Lavinia, is to be given in marriage. You are that man."

"If the gods will it," said Aeneas, "who am I to disagree?"

Latinus had his best horses, bedecked with gilt and splendid trappings, brought for Aeneas as a dowry. Latinus also had a great feast prepared for the Trojans. At that very moment, the goddess Juno, coming back from a trip to Argos, saw how the Trojans were being welcomed by Latinus. She still harbored anger against the Trojans, for the Trojan Paris had chosen Aphrodite as the most beautiful of the goddesses instead of herself.

"Perhaps I can't persuade the hosts of heaven to rid the world of these Trojans," said Juno, "but maybe I can rouse the hosts of hell to make the Trojans pay a princely sum for Paris' perfidy."

Juno sped from heaven to earth. At the entrance to the cave in the valley of Ampsantus, Juno called forth one of the denizens of hell.

"Allecto, goddess of hell," cried Juno, "daughter of night, I ask a boon."

From the cave rose Allecto, a descendant of the Gorgons. Her hair was black and tangled, a nest of vipers hissing and writhing about her face.

"What is it you wish?" asked Allecto.

"You have the power to help me," said Juno. "These Trojans have wronged me, and they will wrong Latinus. You have the power to set even brothers at each other's throats. To pit Latinus' people against these strangers would be a much simpler matter."

"As you wish," said Allecto.

She flew to Latium and entered the palace of Latinus. She made her way to the apartment of the queen, Amata. Allecto bent low over the sleeping woman, plucked a hissing serpent from her hair, and placed

it upon Amata's bosom. The serpent's poisonous venom filled the heart of Amata.

The next day, when Amata sat with Latinus, she brought up the approaching marriage of their daughter.

"Do you think it right that our daughter marry this Trojan?" she asked. "He is homeless. What can he possibly give her? He will take our daughter away from us."

"The oracles have said that Lavinia must marry a foreigner," said Latinus.

"If she must marry a foreigner, she must," said Amata. "But how do you know that this is the right foreigner? You know that the surrounding kingdoms must be considered foreign, for you do not rule them. Is this not so? Prince Turnus, for example, is a foreigner. But we know him. We know his people. How do you know what the oracles mean? Perhaps they are saying you should choose Turnus for our daughter's husband."

"Enough," said Latinus. "I have chosen our daughter's husband."

Amata, with the women of her household, took Lavinia and fled the city. In the forests, she dedicated Lavinia to the god Bacchus. Other women came to join her. They loosed their hair and wore tiger skins. They danced to honor Bacchus.

Allecto wasn't still. She watched with approval at what her poisonous serpent had achieved. She then sped to Prince Turnus and accosted him in his dreams in the guise of an old woman, a priestess of Juno.

"Turnus!" she cried. "Arm yourself. The kingdom is being given to the Trojans. Latinus takes from you your bride and the dowry that you have paid for in blood."

"You don't know what you're saying, old woman," said Turnus. "Juno will smile on me."

Allecto shed her human form then, and stood before the suddenly cowering Turnus. She set her serpents upon him. Shaking with fright, Turnus awoke. He flew through his household, rousing his men, urging them to arm themselves. He made for Latium.

Allecto sped on. She had roused the women of the king's household to rebellion. She had kindled Prince Turnus' desire for battle. She had only to rouse the Latini themselves.

Tyrrhus was the keeper of the herds of King Latinus. His daughter, Silvia, had raised a stag from a fawn, and now it was a pampered pet. All the farmers in the area knew of the animal and let it roam undisturbed. Silvia would comb and bathe the stag. She wound garlands around its horns. The stag wandered the woods by day and returned to Silvia's stable at night.

Aeneas' son, Iulus, was out hunting with his dogs, when Allecto led the hounds to the stag's scent. They pursued the stag into the open, and Iulus let fly an arrow, which fatally wounded the animal. The stag made its way to the stable and died in Silvia's arms. The farmers, furious at the strangers who had killed the tame beast, took up arms and pursued Iulus, who had to flee to his Trojan comrades for help. The Latin farmers engaged the Trojans in battle near the Trojan ships.

Word came then to Latinus that the peace was shattered.

"So be it," he said. "I will not countenance this evil." And, so saying, he shut himself up in his house, leaving the command of the city to Turnus.

Turnus wasted no time. He set the men to digging trenches, piling up stones, and setting stakes in the ground. He had others dig pits. The war trumpet was sounded. The boys and the women filled gaps in the city's walls. Queen Amata, with the women who served her, rode to the temple. There, with Lavinia, the girl who through no fault of her own was the cause of war, they offered prayers and incense to the gods. They prayed for the downfall of the Trojans.

▰▰ CAMILLA IN BATTLE ▰▰

It was to this prelude to battle that Camilla came, leading her horse troops. All the young men came out to watch her ride by. The married women vied to see her as she passed. She wore a crimson cloak, and her hair was pulled back from her face and held in a clasp of gold. She carried a Lycian quiver across her shoul-

ders and a myrtlewood spear. Her companions wore bronze armor, which sparkled in the sunlight.

"I hear that she can run over the ears of wheat in the field, without bending a single stalk," said a young man to a friend.

"I have heard that she can run across the ocean waves and never wet her foot," answered his friend.

Camilla stopped at the city gate, where Turnus had come to meet her. Camilla and her riders dismounted.

"I have come to offer my services to meet the horse-men of Aeneas and his Etruscan allies. This will free you to oversee the command of the walls of the city," she said.

"You are the glory of Italy," said Turnus. "Thank you for your offer. The gods have surely sent you. Spies tell me that Aeneas' horse troops are advancing. I have been planning an ambush for him. With you here, we are guaranteed a victory."

He took Camilla into his confidence and laid the plan before her. He would take his army to the valley walls,

OPPOSITE: Juno's sacred bird was the peacock. Here, two peacocks draw her to heaven in her chariot. BELOW: Noble Etruscan women had prominent public, though not civic, lives and deaths. The monumental sarcophagus of Larthia Seianti shows an elegant, self-assured matron.

where he could block the mountain pass at both ends. Camilla's cavalry would dispatch the Etruscan horsemen. Camilla agreed and led her troops into position.

Her companions stood at the ready. A shout rang out, and they let fly their spears. The sky was dark with their flight. Horses reared, snorting and whinnying, as the spears found their marks. Horses and their riders went down flailing, and dark blood stained the ground.

Camilla, one breast exposed like the Amazons of yore, was at the battle's heart. She threw her javelins, then, in a second sweep, let fly arrow after arrow. Her three handmaids—Larina, Tulla, and Tarpeia—rode at her side, swinging their battle axes. Many Trojans and their allies fell at the hands of the warrior women.

Ornytus, an Etruscan, rode a small pony into the battle. He wore no armor, only a steer's hide draped across his shoulders and a wolf's head upon his head.

"Do you jest with us?" cried Camilla. "Do you think women can't deal with you?"

She threw her spear and dropped him to the ground.

"A woman's weapon has taken you to join the shades of your fathers," Camilla said. "But you can boast that Camilla killed you."

She turned again to the battle. She cornered a Ligerian.

BELOW: The preservation of Rome itself was its citizens' greatest cult. This Roman funerary stele bears a Greek inscription. OPPOSITE: The confident stance of this statue of a Vestal, from the House of the Vestal Virgins in the Roman Forum, bespeaks the great esteem these priestesses enjoyed.

THE ROMAN WORLD

"Brave, indeed," sneered the warrior. "Sitting up there on your horse, ready to flee at a moment's notice. Why not dismount and fight me like a man?"

Angry, Camilla dismounted, handing her reins to one of her companions. The Ligerian grabbed the reins, leapt into the saddle, and kicked the horse's flanks. The horse bolted, but not so fast that Camilla couldn't grab the bridle. She pulled the Ligerian from the saddle and stabbed him with her sword.

Young Arruns, fighting for the Trojans, kept well out of the fray. He watched Camilla, and saw how she alone fueled the ardor of the Latini in the field. He followed her, keeping his distance, waiting and watching. Chloreus, a priest of Cybele, dressed in armor the color of gold, caught Camilla's eye. She began hunting him as Arruns stalked her. Camilla lost herself in the hunt, watching the prey, not thinking about covering her own back. She prepared to pounce on the priest. Arruns readied his spear. Just as Camilla threw her spear, Arruns came around and cast his. The spear caught Camilla in the breast. Arruns crept away from the battlefield.

All her battle maids dismounted and tried to pull the spear out, but it was caught between Camilla's ribs. Camilla fell from her horse. Her eyes rolled back in her head, and she fought for breath.

"Acca," she whispered.

Acca bent low to hear her whispers.

"Ride swiftly to Turnus. Tell him I am slain and that he and his troops must come to relieve me on the battlefield to defend the town."

A great shout went up when Camilla died. The Trojans and Etruscans rallied. Camilla's ranks broke, discipline was lost, and the Latini were routed. Arruns, sneaking down the hillside, was killed by an arrow from an unseen archer, Diana's maid, Opus. Turnus, seeing the rout, gave up his plans for the ambush and headed for the city. Evening found Aeneas and his troops encamped outside the city gates; Turnus' men were camped nearby. The following day Aeneas and Turnus met in combat. Many men fell. At the end of the day, Aeneas killed Turnus. So it was that the Trojans came to settle in Italy.

IRELAND

CHAPTER VI

Irish women played a larger role in the public sphere than their counterparts did in Virgil's Rome or classical Athens. The island of Ireland was inhabited over time by a number of peoples, among them the Celts. The Celts brought with them from the Caucasus a culture that accorded women a number of rights, including leadership in certain social institutions as well as in battle.

The early Irish myths were recorded by Christian scribes, drawing from earlier oral and visual sources. The earliest manuscripts that we have date from the twelfth century C.E. The earliest written descriptions of the Celts come from Greek and Roman sources—not necessarily the most unbiased reporters. However, all the classical writers made mention of the fact that Celtic women were as bold as the men in battle.

It was only with the advent of Christianity that laws stopped the Irish custom of allowing women to go into battle. The Irish Christian saint Colmcille passed a law in 590 C.E. exempting women from military service. It must not have made much of an impression, for in 697 C.E., Adomnan, another leader of the Irish Christian church, finally forbade women from becoming warriors.

The tales of the Irish women warriors are different from the Greek and Roman stories of the Amazons. For one thing, most do not die in battle. For another, most get to choose their sexual part-

OPPOSITE: The goddess in Ireland had many names, inlcuding Danu (whence the Danube River), Medb, and Bridget, but her three main functions rarely varied: she gave life, nurtured it, and took it.

ners, as do Uathach (Oo-thawk), the daughter of the great woman warrior Scáthach (Skaw-thawk), and Medb (Meth-iv), the warrior queen of Connacht. Men may try to control them, but it is futile, as can be seen in the story of how the Morrígu (Mor-ih-goo), the goddess of war, outwitted the Ulster hero CúChulainn (Koo-HULL-in).

Unlike the Amazons, not all Irish warrior women get involved in hand-to-hand combat with a man, or with another woman, for that matter. The male hero CúChulainn stands as the woman warrior Scáthach's champion against the woman warrior Aífe in "Scáthach Trains CúChulainn." In "The Morrígu Bests CúChulainn," the Morrígu enters the fray only after CúChulainn has refused to have sex with her. She punishes him for his temerity by waging a battle of enchantment against him, even as he battles a Connacht hero at the river's ford.

Also in "The Morrígu Bests CúChulainn," Medb doesn't go into war directly. She marshals the troops, and, using sex (or

the hand of her daughter Finnabair) as an inducement, she keeps the men fighting CúChulainn. Medb often uses sex to control her war leaders, in fact, her sexual relationship with Fergus, the exiled Ulster leader, unmans him. (Fergus loses his sword, a phallic symbol, during their dalliance. Medb's husband, Ailill, has a spy steal it.) This isn't the first time Fergus has been outdone by a female. He was, at one time, the king of Ulster, but because of an unwise marriage with Nes, the mother of his stepson Conchobor (CON-hov-ur), Fergus had lost the throne.

There is some similarity between the Irish and Amazon tales. For example, the sons are sent to the fathers to be raised: Aífe promises to send CúChulainn's son, Connla, to him at the end of seven years. The daughters, however, stay with their mothers, as can be seen in the relationships between Medb and Finnabair and Scáthach and Uathach. What's more, the mothers control the sexuality of their daughters. Medb promises Finnabair to any warrior who will fight CúChulainn. Scáthach gives her consent for Uathach to bed CúChulainn.

Some Irish warrior women, like the Amazons of the Classical world, are to be found at the very edge of the known world.

SCÁTHACH TRAINS CÚCHULAINN

CúChulainn, the young champion, was without a wife, which troubled the men of Ulster, for CúChulainn was fair of face and the greatest warrior in the province. All the young girls admired him, and the married women watched him as he practiced his warrior arts on the green in front of Emain Macha (Ev-in MA-hah), the royal fort of Ulster. The warriors spoke to King Conchobor of their unease at CúChulainn's unmarried state.

"A woman will have to be found for CúChulainn," said one.

Thus, Scáthach, Uathach, and Aife are from Alba (today's Scotland). Others, however, such as Medb and the Morrígu, live and breathe in the very heart of Ireland.

The following stories are taken from the *Táin Bó Cuailnge* (The Cattle Raid of Cooley), the oldest Western European vernacular epic. The *Táin Bó Cuailnge* centers on CúChulainn, the male hero; there are few stories from the female perspective, perhaps because male Christian scribes recorded the stories. There are, however, strong female characters who reveal the physical, emotional, and intellectual power of women in the stories, and these are the heroines of Irish myths.

"Indeed, the passion of the women of Ulster for CúChulainn is not something to take lightly," said another.

"A woman of his own will keep him occupied," said the first.

"If he is occupied, he will be less likely to ruin our daughters or steal our wives," said the second.

Conchobor gave them a skeptical look.

"Also consider, Conchobor, what would happen if the warrior were to die young," said the first.

"It would be tragic, it would," said the second. "Ulster will never see his like again, unless it is the son of CúChulainn."

Conchobor gave this some thought. It was important that CúChulainn produce an heir.

"You are right," he agreed at last. He called for messengers and sent them to all the provinces of Ireland to seek a suitable woman for the young warrior.

In the meantime, CúChulainn heard of a beautiful young woman named Emer (Aye-vir) who lived in the gardens of the god Lug (Lew). CúChulainn and his charioteer, Laeg (Loy-gh), drove to Lug's garden. They found Emer on the grassy plain with her female guard of fifty foster sisters. The young women were practicing the arts of embroidery and fine stitching; Emer looked up from her stitching as the young men approached. She had heard of the young warrior, and she recognized him immediately from the descriptions she had heard. She found his face fair.

"May the road rise to meet you," said Emer, in a traditional Irish greeting.

"May you see only good things," said CúChulainn, blessing Emer in return.

Emer's face flushed. CúChulainn, from his vantage point in the chariot, could see down the top of her dress. He raised his eyes to hers.

"Now *there's* a sweet land where I would travel," he said admiringly.

Emer looked him in the eye. She had regained her composure.

"No man will travel this country until he has killed a man at every ford," she said coolly.

"Then shall I travel that pleasant country," said CúChulainn.

Emer's foster sisters looked at each other.

Emer laughed. "No man will travel here until he has fought three groups of nine men each, carrying twice his own weight in gold. Each group must be killed with one stroke, and the middle man in each group of nine must be unharmed."

"Then shall I travel that most pleasant land," said CúChulainn.

"No man will travel here unless he has gone sleepless for an entire year," said Emer.

"It shall be so," said CúChulainn.

He and Laeg returned to Emain Macha that evening. Emer's foster sisters marveled at the bold talk, and they told their fathers about the riddles that passed between Emer and CúChulainn.

Word of the exchange reached Emer's father, Forgall. From the description the girls gave, he knew that the young man in the chariot had been CúChulainn from Emain Macha. Forgall made up his mind to send the young warrior far away, where, he hoped,

BELOW: The Irish Celts fought with short swords and spears. Myths and tombs tell of warriors riding to battle in chariots, from which they dismounted to engage in hand-to-hand combat. OPPOSITE: The Celts may have named their armor, including shields like this bronze one, found in a sacrifical hoard in London's Thames River.

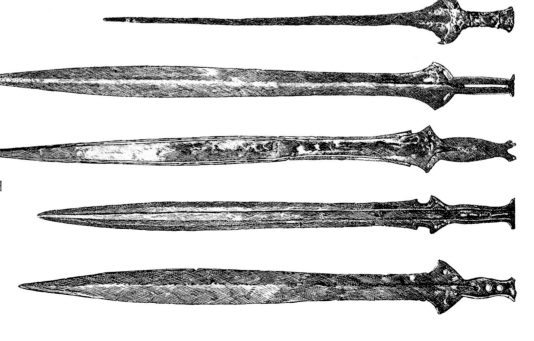

CúChulainn would be killed, for Forgall had been told that the wild young warrior who came for Emer's hand would kill him.

The very next day, Forgall dressed in the clothes of one who came from Gaul (present–day France) and made his way to Conchobor's court at Emain Macha. Saying he came from the land of Gaul to pay tribute to Conchobor, Forgall lavished rich gifts on Conchobor and flattered the prowess of his warriors. At last, the king and Forgall sat alone.

"Your nephew, CúChulainn, shows great promise as a warrior," said Forgall.

"Promise?" said Conchobor. "I should say he *is* a great warrior."

"Great he is," said Forgall, "but his abilities would be unsurpassed if only he studied with the likes of the great Domnall Mildemail in Scotland, or Scáthach, the great woman warrior. Yes, indeed, if only he could study with those two great warriors, no one in Europe could beat him."

CúChulainn heard of Forgall's discussion with Conchobor. He decided to go to study in Scotland. He announced his decision to his Uncle Conchobor as the king sat with Forgall.

"Don't waste any time, young man," said Forgall. "You should go immediately."

"I will go tomorrow," said CúChulainn.

The next morning, CúChulainn left for Scotland. He stopped to see Emer, to tell her where he was going. They pledged to be true to each other.

"Be on guard," she said. "That was no Gaul but my father, Forgall. He will see you destroyed rather than married to me."

CúChulainn took his leave. He traveled to the east until he arrived in Scotland, where he studied with Domnall. Domnall taught him many warrior's feats, such as how to walk on hot coals without burning his feet and how to walk on the points of spears without making his feet bleed.

"Young CúChulainn," said Domnall, "your training with me is complete, but you really should travel farther east. Scáthach, the shadowy one, will complete your training as a warrior."

CúChulainn traveled to eastern Scotland; at last, he came to a camp beside a wide river. There were many young warriors in the camp.

"I have come to study with Scáthach, the shadowy one," said CúChulainn. "Do you know where I might find her?"

"We are the shadowy one's pupils," said a young warrior. "You will find her on the island in the middle of the river."

"How do I cross to the island?" asked CúChulainn.

"By the pupils' bridge," said the young man. "No one can travel the bridge who hasn't been trained. It will throw you upon your back should you make the attempt."

CúChulainn tried to cross the bridge three times. Each time, he no sooner reached the midway point than the bridge's far end flew upward, toppling him backward. The young warriors had gathered round to watch his attempts. Now they hooted with laughter.

CúChulainn's warrior anger filled him. His face flushed. His hair stood on end. He ran to the bridge, leapt to the midway point in the bridge, then leapt again before the bridge had a chance to spring up against him. He walked boldly to the gate of Scáthach's fort and struck

the wooden door with his spear so hard that the spear pierced through to the other side.

"Mistress!" cried the gatekeeper, hurrying into Scáthach's presence. "Someone has thrown a spear through the front gate."

"Obviously," said Scáthach, "this is a warrior who has had complete training elsewhere."

Scáthach turned to her daughter, Uathach, who sat beside her at the fireside.

"Go, see who this young man is," she commanded.

Uathach went to the front gate and looked over the wall at CúChulainn. The sight of him pleased her greatly. She returned to her mother.

"The young man has a warrior's build. He is fair of face and looks as though he comes from good stock," said Uathach to her mother.

"Indeed," said her mother, "he pleases you."

"He does," affirmed Uathach.

"Take him to bed tonight, if that is your wish," said Scáthach.

"If he would like to, I would not protest," said Uathach.

Uathach returned to the gate and let CúChulainn in.

"Follow me, my lord," said Uathach, pretending to be a serving girl. "My mistress has sent me to see to your needs."

She brought water to bathe CúChulainn. She brought him food. CúChulainn, thinking her a servant girl, grabbed her and tried to pull her down on the bed.

She cried out, because he hurt her finger while doing so. Her cry roused the house guards. Cochar Cruibne rushed CúChulainn and tried to best the young man, but CúChulainn parried all his thrusts. At last, CúChulainn killed Cochar and beheaded him. Scáthach mourned at that, for Cochar had served her well for many years.

"I apologize for grieving you," said CúChulainn.

"Who will guard my house?" asked Scáthach.

"I will take over the duties of the dead man. I will lead your armies and be your champion," said CúChulainn.

"Agreed," said Scáthach.

Uathach stayed with CúChulainn for three days.

"If you really want to learn to be a hero," said Uathach on the third day, "I can tell you how to get my mother to agree to train you."

"How?" asked CúChulainn.

"She is teaching my two brothers, Cuar [Koo-ur] and Cat [Cut], the secrets of heroic deeds," said Uathach.

"Tell me where she is, and I will go to her," said CúChulainn.

"It isn't that simple," said Uathach. "She will not train you as her son unless you demand it."

OPPOSITE: Places of water, often worshiped as goddesses, were particularly sacred in ancient Ireland. ABOVE: The sun wheel is carved on an Irish quern stone, used to grind grain.

"Tell me what I must do," said CúChulainn.

"You will find her in the great yew tree, sitting atop the weapons chest. You must leap into the tree and put your sword to her breast and make her promise three things—thoroughness in training, a dowry for marriage, and insight into your future," said Uathach.

CúChulainn did as Uathach advised. He found Scáthach in the great yew tree. He leapt into the tree and held the naked blade of his sword against her breast.

"I will kill you," he said.

"I will give you three wishes if you do not harm me, if you can state them in one breath," said Scáthach.

"You must give me thoroughness in training, a dowry for marriage, and insight into my future," said CúChulainn.

So it was that CúChulainn was welcomed at Scáthach's fort, and she trained him in great deeds and the warrior's craft. Uathach, her daughter, lived with the young warrior. CúChulainn scarcely thought of Emer, who remained true to her vows.

SCÁTHACH'S BATTLE WITH AIFE

Scáthach, the shadowy one, taught the young warrior CúChulainn many feats. She taught him to juggle nine apples at once. She taught him how to balance on a rope while swordfighting. She taught him how to leap through the air like a salmon swimming upstream, how to step on a lance in midflight, how to truss a warrior on the points of spears, and how to avoid the poisoned stroke. She taught him many other things as well, including secret weapons and secret words. During his training, CúChulainn lived with Uathach, Scáthach's daughter, and continued to serve as Scáthach's personal champion.

The woman warrior Aife (Ee-fee) marched against Scáthach. Scáthach rallied her warriors and set out to meet Aife at the river's ford. Their two armies drew up and faced each other, one on each side of the river.

Scáthach feared for CúChulainn's safety in the coming battle because he knew no fear and was always to be found in the thick of battle, so she put a sleeping draft in his food. When he fell asleep beside the fire, she tied him up and left him on the couch. She went out to face her enemy.

The battle had no sooner begun than CúChulainn sat bolt upright on the couch. The sleeping draft that would have kept a lesser man under its influence for twenty-four hours had worn off in less than one. CúChulainn joined Scáthach's two sons, Cuar and Cat, on the battlefield. They faced three of Aife's warriors.

Two of the warriors carried the same names as Scáthach's sons—Cuar and Cat. So, Cuar was to battle Cuar, and Cat to battle Cat. CúChulainn sped ahead of his brothers in battle, and killed the third, Crufe, as well as Cuar and Cat.

Evening came on, and the armies retired for the night. As soon as the sun rose the next day, the two armies took the field once more. Three of Aife's warriors challenged the two sons of Scáthach. These three warriors were the sons of Eis, the bird-headed woman, and their names were Ciri, Biri, and Blaicne. They challenged Scáthach's sons to battle while doing the rope feat.

This required great skill. A rope tied to two large boulders was stretched taut a foot off the ground. Aife's warriors mounted the rope and prepared to do battle.

"This does not bode well," mused Scáthach.

"You have trained us well, mother," said Cuar.

"We are up to the challenge, mother," said Cat.

"It pains me to say it, but Aife is a harder warrior than I," said Scáthach. "I fear she has taught her warriors things that I haven't taught you. Plus there are three of them and only two of you."

"Have no fear, Scáthach," said CúChulainn. "The task is mine."

CúChulainn leapt onto the rope before Scáthach's sons could. Keeping his balance easily, he killed all three of Aife's warriors. Aife was filled with rage. This young warrior had killed six of her greatest warriors in just two days. She decided to end the battle decisively.

"What is this, Scáthach? You let a stranger fight your battles for you? Where is your womanly courage?" Aife taunted as CúChulainn stepped down off the rope.

"What is it you wish?" asked Scáthach.

OPPOSITE: The fluid lines of Celtic design may have protected the wearer of this hard-used bronze helmet. LEFT: Gerald of Wales complained in his book on Ireland that all the Irish carried axes, and that if you looked at them sideways, they would split your head. Double-headed axes were traditionally associated with goddesses.

"Do you have the courage to join me in single combat?" sneered Aife.

"I accept your challenge, woman," said CúChulainn, stepping forward. "I am Scáthach's champion." He turned and conferred with Scáthach in secret. "What is it that Aife values most?"

"That is easily answered," said Scáthach. "Her two horses, her chariot, and her charioteer are nearest to Aife's heart."

Aife jumped onto the rope. CúChulainn joined her. They drew their swords. Aife, ferocious in her fury, forced CúChulainn to give ground. She kept him off balance with her attack. She struck so hard that sparks flew from their swords as they clanged together. CúChulainn retreated further. Aife slashed at

CúChulainn. He parried her swift, sure strokes, but the woman warrior was winning. The metal of the swords shrieked. CúChulainn's sword shattered in his hand. Aife had left him with only the hilt.

"Great tragedy, Aife!" exclaimed CúChulainn. "Look. Your two horses have bolted at the sound of the breaking metal. They have plunged over the cliff. Your horses and your charioteer are all dead. Your fine chariot is demolished."

Even though Aife knew he lied, she hesitated, and for a moment, she sought to catch a glance of her beloved horses and chariot. CúChulainn took advantage of her hesitation and leapt upon her. He seized her by her breasts and tossed her over his shoulder like a sack of grain. He carried her to Scáthach, threw her onto the ground at Scáthach's feet and, grabbing a sword from Cuar, held the naked blade to Aife's chest.

"Spare my life, CúChulainn," Aife pleaded.

"Give me three wishes," demanded CúChulainn, his sword gleaming fiercely in the sun.

"Whatever you can ask in one breath, you may have," said Aife.

"You will provide hostages for Scáthach, and your promise never to attack her again; you will sleep with me tonight at your own fort; and you will bear me a son," said CúChulainn.

"It shall be so," said Aife.

CúChulainn spent the night with Aife. It didn't take long before Aife announced that she was with child, prophesying that she would bear a son.

LEFT: This imposing Celtic earth goddess wears a torc, a necklace worn by women and men, and believed by some to refer to the crescent moon. Celtic deities were sometimes universal, as here, while at other times they were embodied as specific places.

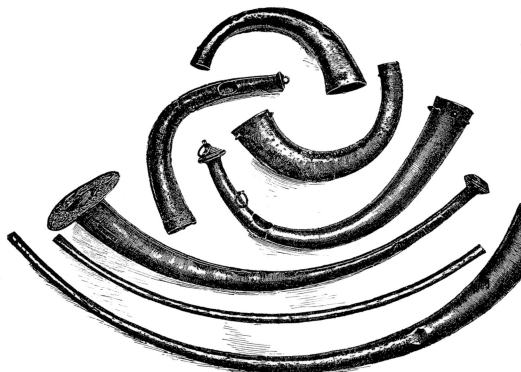

CúChulainn stood to the side, using his toes to cling to the path, fearful of falling into the crashing sea far below. The old woman stabbed viciously at his toes with her staff as she crept past. CúChulainn had seen her blow coming, and he leapt high into the air. Coming down behind her on the path, he beheaded the one-eyed old woman. In reality, the murderous crone was Eis, the bird-headed woman, mother of the last three warriors CúChulainn had slain, though he did not know this; he beheaded her because she attacked him.

Upon his return to her camp, Scáthach tended CúChulainn's wounds. She took Aife's hostages and returned to her own country.

When CúChulainn's strength had returned, word came from Conchobor that he should return to Ulster. He prepared to leave, and Scáthach gave him then the last of the three wishes she had granted him: insight into his future.

"You will face many foes, and you will destroy Cruachan's heroes. You will be made to bleed. Your country will be in bondage, your cattle will be stolen. Men in Scotland will hear of your fame. Many women will love your bright body. Aife and Uathach will mourn your broken, lifeless body when you are thirty-three," foretold Scáthach.

CúChulainn returned to his uncle, Conchobor. Back in his homeland, he regaled the men of Ulster with tales of his exploits.

"Seven years from now, I will send the boy to you for his patrimony," said Aife. "But you must leave a name for him."

"His name shall be Connla," said CúChulainn. He left a gold thumb-ring for the boy. "Tell him to seek me when his finger fits this ring. He must not reveal his name to anyone. He must not make way for any man. He must refuse no man combat."

CúChulainn left Aife then and made his way back to Scáthach's camp. On his return, he met a one-eyed old woman on the path that wound along the cliff's edge, an evil portent. The ocean pounded the rocks below.

"Out of my way," snarled the old woman.

"There is no room to pass," said CúChulainn.

"What do you expect an old woman to do?" she asked. "I am too old to climb upon the rocks."

THE MORRIGU BESTS CÚCHULAINN

Medb, queen of Connacht, argued with her husband, Ailill. Both sought to prove that they had brought more wealth to the marriage than the other. They counted everything they owned—armaments, gold, silver, fine fabrics, horses, and cattle. They were equal in all things, save one. Medb lacked a bull as fine as that of Ailill.

Stung, Medb sent out messengers, searching for a prize bull. She found such a bull in Ulster, but its owner, offended at her brash request for the animal, refused to give it to her. So she decided to take it.

Medb rallied the troops of Connacht and marched on Ulster. Ailill accompanied her with his army. With them rode the mercenaries of Ulster, led by Fergus. Medb was worried about their loyalty, and with good reason. Fergus had been king of Ulster, but had been ousted by his stepson, Conchobor. This alone would not have set Fergus against his people, but Conchobor, using treachery, had been responsible for the death of Fergus' son. Thus, it was an act of retaliation when Fergus went to war against Conchobor.

Medb's army sent small war parties throughout Ulster, each group returning with spoils of war. The cows and slaves they captured filled the invading warriors' camp.

"We can't all take the same road," said Medb to Ailill. "We must divide the army. We will move too slowly as one."

"What do you suggest?" asked Ailill.

"You can take half by way of the Midluachair road," she said. "I'll take Fergus. We'll go through the mountains by way of Bernas Bo Ulad."

"That will be difficult," said Fergus. "We'll need to cut a path through the mountain to get the cattle and goods through."

"It may take a little time," said Medb, "but the journey should be worth our while."

"We'll do as you suggest, Medb," said Ailill. As he left Medb, Ailill took his charioteer aside.

"Ferloga, you must be my eyes and ears," said Ailill. "I wonder what Medb is about. Keep your eye on Fergus and her."

"I will watch them closely," said Ferloga.

So Ferloga went with Medb's half of the army. He watched Medb, but she did not know she was being watched. He noted that she leaned close to whisper in Fergus' ear several times. The army moved slowly up the mountainside. Medb dropped back, giving orders and urging speed. Ferloga noticed that Fergus was no longer at the head of the column. Ferloga turned back. He could no longer see either Medb or Fergus. He backtracked, moving slowly lest anyone suspect that he spied for Ailill.

Ferloga found the couple at Cluithre, wrapped in each other's embrace, naked on the grass. He hid his horses and moved closer on foot. Fergus' sword lay forgotten near a grove of trees. Ferloga crept up and stole Fergus' sword from its scabbard. He carved a wooden sword and placed it in the scabbard, then made his way back to his horses. He hurried to meet Ailill's half of the army.

"Did you see anything?" asked Ailill.

"I found them in each other's arms, as you feared," said Ferloga. He handed Fergus' sword to Ailill.

Ailill grinned at him. Ferloga grinned back.

"Well done," said Ailill. "I suppose she's justified. She worries that he will not be loyal, that he will balk at waging war on his stepson, Conchobor."

Ailill handed Fergus' sword to Ferloga.

"Take good care of Fergus' sword," Ailill said. "Wrap it well and hide it under your chariot seat."

Meanwhile, Medb and Fergus, finished with love-making, slept on the grassy knoll until the lowering of the sun woke them. They dressed hurriedly. Fergus belted on his scabbard, then discovered that his sword was gone, a wooden toy in its place.

"This can't be," said Fergus, bewildered.

"What's wrong?" asked Medb.

Fergus searched the woods but couldn't find his sword. He returned to Medb then and urged a return to the army, worried that they would be caught far from the protecting forces when darkness fell.

The two halves of the army had come together on an open plain by the time Fergus and Medb caught up. Ailill sent Ferloga to Fergus with a message.

"Ailill asks that you join him for a game of chess," said Ferloga.

"I'll be there shortly," said Fergus.

Ailill laughed loudly as Fergus entered the tent.

"What's so funny?" asked Fergus.

"Oh, nothing," said Ailill. "It's just that you look as though Medb took you on a hard ride."

"What do you mean by that?" asked Fergus.

"Oh, nothing," said Ailill. "Those heights where Medb led you today must have required a lot of physical stamina."

"Cutting a pass through the mountain was difficult," said Fergus guardedly.

Ailill laughed again. "I can imagine it would be difficult, indeed, to burrow into the belly of a such a majestic mountain. The task requires a man who is up to a challenge. But sit, let's play chess."

Fergus ran his hand over the wooden hilt of his toy sword and looked closely at Ailill. But Ailill avoided his gaze, placing his chess pieces on the board. He held up one of the pieces.

"Don't you think this queen is lovely?" he asked.

"Indeed," said Fergus.

Ailill looked fiercely at Fergus. "Don't think you'll win her," he said. "I have no intention of losing."

Fergus blushed as he took his seat. They played the game, but Fergus played poorly.

The next morning the advance scouts told of a terrible warrior at the river's ford ahead. He had done mighty deeds, and the morning was still young. He had slain all those in the scouting party, except the one who had escaped to raise the alarm.

"Who can this be, this great warrior?" asked Medb. "Describe him for Fergus," she commanded the scout. "Perhaps he will know this terrible warrior."

"He is young," replied the scout. "A boy, really. He hasn't even got a beard."

"I do know him," said Fergus. "That is CúChulainn, the greatest warrior of Ulster, perhaps the greatest of all Ireland. He will exact a terrible toll on our forces."

"What can one boy do against such a mighty force?" asked Medb. "Or are you afraid to face one of your own? Is this a bastard son?"

"I am afraid of no one," said Fergus. "But CúChulainn is a mighty warrior. He has learned magic arts as well. He can control the very rivers."

"So, you will not face this warrior. I thought not," said Medb. "What could I possibly have expected from one who has betrayed his own?"

"Spare me your sharp tongue, Medb," snapped Fergus. "But you are right about one thing, I'll not raise another blow against my own people for the likes of you."

Medb turned her back to him and called to her troops. "Is there no one to face this beardless boy? Are there no men among you?"

Ailill's son, Maine, came forward then with his troop of thirty men. They advanced against CúChulainn, but the great Ulster warrior killed every single one, including Maine. This angered Medb's men, and they sent another troop against the boy. CúChulainn killed them all.

"At this rate," said Ailill, "this boy warrior will destroy our entire army. We must do something."

"What do you suggest?" said Medb.

"I will send a messenger, Mac Roth, to tell the boy I will pay whatever he asks if he will serve me."

Mac Roth took the message to CúChulainn, but the boy refused to turn his allegiance from his uncle, Conchobor. "There is one thing that might do," granted CúChulainn, "if your king will agree to it."

"Tell me your demand," said Mac Roth.

"I will cease to rain terror on your army, if, one by one, the greatest warriors of Connacht agree to fight me at the ford," said CúChulainn.

"I will deliver your message," said Mac Roth.

Ailill agreed to CúChulainn's request, hoping that losing only one man a day would buy him time to find a solution. So each day one of the great warriors of Connacht faced CúChulainn at the ford of the river. He killed so many that soon no one wanted to face him. Medb promised her daughter to whoever could overcome the boy warrior. When that didn't work, she offered herself. When that didn't work, she shamed champions into going against him.

At the same time, Medb plotted to turn the events to her advantage. While CúChulainn was occupied, she took her half of the army into Ulster and raided the countryside, laying it to waste. She looked for the bull that had brought her on her quest. She attacked the woman Finnmor, the Ulster warrior Celtchar's wife, taking fifty servant women from her.

Back at the river's ford, CúChulainn destroyed all who came against him, including his foster brother, Ferdia. The battles took their toll, however, and he was covered with gashes and other fearsome wounds. His strength was slowly draining away. It was then that a beautiful woman came to him.

"Who are you?" he asked.

"I am the daughter of a king," she answered. "I have come to offer myself to you, with my treasure and my cattle. I have heard great things about you."

"This isn't a good time," said CúChulainn. "I don't have time for a woman right now."

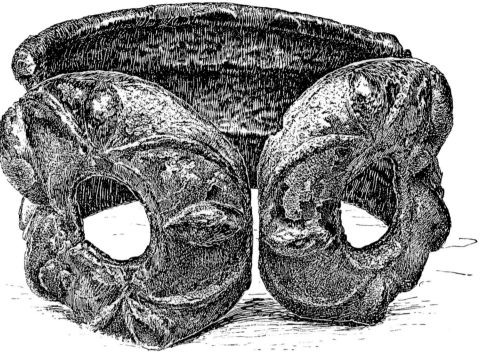

"Perhaps I can help you," said the woman.

"There is no time for the repose you offer," said CúChulainn.

The woman's face flushed with anger. She was no longer beautiful. "Then I will hinder," she said. "When things are going badly for you, I'll make them worse. If you fight in the river, I'll come against you as an eel and trip you."

"I didn't think you looked like a king's daughter," said CúChulainn. "I see you for what you really are. You are the Morrigu, the goddess of war. If you come against me as an eel, seeking to trip me when I am fighting, I shall have to break your ribs, a mark you'll carry forever, unless I remove it."

"Then I'll come against you as a she-wolf, stampeding your horses into the ford," she said.

"Then I'll put a slingstone through your eye," said CúChulainn, "a mark you'll carry forever, unless I remove it."

"Then I'll come change myself into a red heifer, and I will lead the cattle herd into the ford to trample you," the woman said.

"Then I'll break your leg with a stone," CúChulainn said, "a mark you'll carry forever, unless I remove it."

Now that he had heard her threats, CúChulainn didn't fear the Morrigu, for he was young and full of himself. The Morrigu left, vanishing into the air.

The Connacht hero Loch challenged CúChulainn to personal combat at the ford the next day. Loch hoped to avenge his brother, whom CúChulainn had killed on the previous day. On foot, with only their swords for weapons, in the middle of the water, they slashed and hacked at each other.

The Morrigu seized her chance and slipped into the water in the shape of an eel. When Loch was pressing CúChulainn the hardest, she wrapped herself in three coils around CúChulainn's legs, tripping him.

CúChulainn fell backwards, into the water. Fergus, on the riverbank, was concerned.

"A terrible thing, this," said Fergus, "to have the greatest champion of Ulster on his backside in the water like a schoolboy. He will shame Ulster in front of the men of Connacht if he dies in such a position."

Fergus turned to the druid Bricriu, who stood beside him. Lijke all druids, Bricriu was a satirist who controlled the power of words and whose words could create or destroy, or shame a warrior into action.

"Do something," Fergus said.

Bricriu strode nearer the water's edge. "Some warrior you are, CúChulainn. You shame the men of Ulster in your clumsiness. Can't you keep your balance when a little salmon swims by?"

CúChulainn's cheeks flushed with shame. He struck the eel hard, smashing its ribs. The Morrigu released her grip and slipped away. She made her way to the river's bank and shifted into the shape of a gray she-wolf. She slunk along in the tall grass, coming up behind the herd of stolen cattle grazing nearby. She sprang at the cattle. They bellowed and began to run. The herd stampeded into the river, nearly trampling CúChulainn and Loch, the Connacht warrior. The Morrigu ran after the cattle, nipping at their flanks.

CúChulainn took his slingshot and hurled a stone at the Morrigu. It struck her eye out. The Morrigu dove into the midst of the cattle herd and shifted from the shape of a she-wolf to that of a red heifer. CúChulainn lost sight of his wily enemy. In the shape of a heifer, the Morrigu led the stampeding cattle directly at CúChulainn. CúChulainn used his slingshot to hurl a stone at the red heifer. The missile broke the heifer's leg. The Morrigu limped away, changing her shape yet again into that of a carrion-eating crow, and flying to safety.

Loch struck at CúChulainn with renewed vigor. The two warriors fought hard and long in the water at

ABOVE: The Irish goddess Macha built the ditch at Emain Macha with the pin from a brooch that might have resembled this splendid piece. OPPOSITE: Horses were prominent in Irish culture, and the horse-goddess Epona was an important Celtic deity.

the ford. CúChulainn's charioteer, Laeg, floated a special spear upon the water to CúChulainn. The boy warrior grabbed it and stabbed Loch in the groin, the only part of the Connacht warrior not covered by horn armor. Loch pitched face forward into the water, and CúChulainn cut off his head.

CúChulainn was greatly wearied after the daylong duel. The Morrigu had hurt him, and Loch had been a valiant opponent. Chilled to the bone from the cold waters of the river, he climbed stiffly up the riverbank. Not far from the river he saw a hunchbacked, one-eyed old woman milking a cow.

"Old woman, I faint from hunger. Give me some milk from your cow," he asked, "and you shall be blessed."

The old woman pulled milk from one teat and gave it to the boy warrior. He drank it greedily.

"May you be hale and hearty," said CúChulainn.

Suddenly, the old woman's hunched back was straightened, and she no longer breathed with a rasp. She smiled.

"The milk has taken the edge off my hunger, but I desire more," said CúChulainn.

The old woman pulled milk from the second teat and gave it to CúChulainn. He drank it down.

"The milk gives me new life," said CúChulainn. "May you be as renewed as I from the giving."

The old woman's blind eye was suddenly restored. Her eyes twinkled with the clarity of youth.

"Just one more draft," asked CúChulainn, "and I shall be as strong as ever."

The old woman milked the third teat and CúChulainn drank the milk down as quickly as the first two drafts. He wiped his mouth with the back of his hand.

"That has restored me," said CúChulainn. "May the giving restore you as well."

The old woman stood and her crooked legs were straightened. She assumed the aspect of the young woman who had offered herself to CúChulainn.

"You have healed me," said the Morrigu, and she laughed.

"I wouldn't have if I had known it to be you," said CúChulainn.

The Morrigu assumed the shape of a carrion-eating crow and flew away. She lit in a tree out of CúChulainn's range of shot and cackled and cawed, jeering at the hero she had outwitted.

WARRIOR WOMEN OF THE BIBLE

Throughout the Old Testament, a number of women of power and personality—beginning with Eve—precipitate or change events, sometimes for the better, sometimes for the worse. The women of the New Testament, a document of the New Law, based on love, if not pacifism, are courageous and strong, but not militant, like their sisters of the old order. Deborah, Jael, and Judith are, above all, patriots, who leave their daily lives to enter the arena of politics and war, not to mention murder, out of love for their nation. Deborah and Judith direct men in battle. Because their people were united in the worship of a common god, these women are examples of militant piety, as well as patriotism. As in war, their devotion to their homeland justifies breaking the commandment against murder.

The exploits of Deborah, who lived around the twelfth century B.C.E., are recorded in the Book of Judges, believed to be the oldest part of the Bible. She is a prophet and a judge in Israel; it is her place to sit by the side of the road and settle disputes. This position demonstrates that the society of the Israelites made a place for the spiritually evolved, both female and male, just as Greek society of a later time revered and feared its priestesses, though denying women a civic identity. Deborah's part is to prophesy to the army, thus communicating God's strategy to them.

OPPOSITE: Artemisia Gentileschi's masterful use of shadow and light accentuates the emotions implicit in Judith's murder of Holofernes in one of several paintings she made on the subject in the first half of the seventeenth century.

Jael is a housewife—or rather a tent-wife, since she and her husband belong to a tribe of nomads. Cool, pragmatic, and ruthless, she uses the tools at hand, including her traditional female role, to achieve her purpose, taking up where Deborah left off. Judith, who may enjoy more freedom because of her widowhood and her wealth, goes into the enemy camp, into the tent of Holofernes himself, her reputation shielded by her religious devotion and her virtue. Like Deborah and Jael, Judith displays none of the girlish hesitation, seductiveness, or sentimentality that would make her tale an engaging movie of the week today.

Some of the most famous women of the Bible are bad women, such as Jezebel and Delilah. Jezebel, married to a king of Israel in the ninth century B.C.E., was a Phoenician princess, a powerful woman who brought paganism, including the worship of Baal, into Israel and persecuted the prophets. Delilah—like Deborah and Jael, a figure in the Book of Judges—uses the power of her sexuality, like Judith, to political ends. Unlike Judith, Delilah cedes her virtue, by becoming Samson's lover.

The heroines Deborah, Jael, and Judith display none of the behavior that many societies consider desirable for women; they are neither shy nor dithering. The one who comes the closest to being nice—the feminine quality par excellence—is Deborah, who reminds Barak that if he follows her—that is, God's—counsel, he will receive "no glory," for God "will give the enemy into the hands of a woman."

JAEL FREES ISRAEL

Jabin, king of the Canaanites, subjugated the Israelites. He put Sisera, the commander-in-chief of his armed forces, in charge of the defeated Israelites. Sisera was a harsh taskmaster, and he ruled Israel with an iron fist for twenty years.

During that time, there was a wise woman named Deborah who sat beneath a palm tree on the road between Ramah and Bethel, two villages in Israel. Everyone came to her for justice, for she was both a prophet and the judge of Israel. One day she sent for Barak, a man with military training, for she had a message for him from the god of Israel. Barak came to her and listened to her counsel.

"You must raise an army of ten thousand men from the tribes of Naphtali and Zebulun," Deborah said. "The Lord will draw Sisera with his nine hundred chariots to the Kishon River. There, the Lord will use Sisera's overweening confidence in his superior weapons to crush him. At the foot of Mount Tabor, the Lord will deliver Sisera into your hands."

"I will not do this thing unless you come with me," said Barak.

"Certainly, I will come," said Deborah. "But this will give you no glory. For instead of the Lord giving the enemy into your hands, he will give the enemy into the hands of a woman."

Deborah traveled with Barak to the tribes of Naphtali and Zebulun, where Barak raised an army of ten thousand men. The army headed for Mount Tabor, near the Kishon River. Sisera heard that Barak had raised an army, and his spies brought him word that the army was encamped near Mount Tabor. The military governor mustered his nine hundred chariots and his fighting men and headed for the Kishon.

Deborah summoned Barak to her and said, "Sisera comes with his nine hundred chariots and his fighting men. Now will the Lord deliver him into your hands."

From the heights of Mount Tabor, Barak and his army charged down upon the nine hundred chariots and the fighting men of Sisera. Sisera's chariots couldn't

retreat because the Kishon River barred their way. His fighting men were trapped between Barak's army, the mountain heights, and the surging river. Barak's army quickly won.

Sisera leapt from his chariot and ran on foot into the wilderness, abandoning his army in his terror. Barak pursued the chariots until he had caught them all, and then he put all of Sisera's soldiers to the sword. Sisera was afraid. He thought to find an ally. Knowing that Heber, an ally of Jabin, the king of the Canaanites, was settled nearby, Sisera ran to the tent of Jael, Heber's wife.

"You are welcome, my lord," said Jael. "You have found sanctuary here. Come in. Don't be afraid. I will hide you."

She took Sisera into her tent.

"Give me water," he said. "I die of thirst."

He listened for sounds of pursuers. "If anyone comes, tell them you haven't seen me," he said.

Jael, who secretly supported the Israelites, assured Sisera that he was safe with her. She gave him water and milk to drink, then covered him with a rug. Soon she heard his snores. She took up a tent peg and a hammer, crept up to him, and hammered the peg into his temple, killing him.

Barak, searching all the neighborhood for Sisera, came upon Jael's tent. She went out to meet him.

"I am searching for the enemy of Israel," said Barak. "Have you seen him?"

"Come," said Jael, "I will show you the man you seek."

Jael led him into her tent and showed him Sisera, lying dead with the tent peg through his temple.

"The Lord is good to me," said Barak. "Blessed be Jael. Blessed be she above all women in the tents, for she has struck down Sisera, the enemy of Israel."

That day Barak and Deborah gave thanks to the god of Israel and sang a song to Jael, praising her.

JUDITH SLAYS HOLOFERNES

When Nebuchadnezzar was king of Assyria, he called his general, Holofernes, to him and commanded that he march on the peoples to the west, including the Israelites.

"Take one hundred twenty thousand infantry and twelve thousand mounted archers," said Nebuchadnezzar. "Conquer the land to the west. Those who surrender, hold them for me until I decide their fate. If any will not surrender, kill them. Let the bodies fill the river valleys and choke the streams."

"I will do as you command, my king," said Holofernes.

Holofernes marshaled the infantry and the mounted archers. He gathered camels, asses, and mules to carry the baggage. He took sheep, oxen, goats, and other animals for food for all the men. He took gold and silver from the royal treasury to pay his army. The dust from his cavalcade filled the heavens as Holofernes and his

BELOW: The artist, Jacopo Palma the Younger, gave his Judith the face and gesture of an avenging angel. The use of light and dark enhance the scene's gory drama. OPPOSITE: Antoine Dufour's *Lives of Famous Women* gives pride of place to Judith's crosslike sword, perhaps to counter resemblances between Judith and Salome.

vast army marched toward the west. They conquered all the towns in their path. Those that would not surrender, Holofernes treated harshly, burning their wheat and murdering their young men.

From Tyre to Sidon to Damascus, word spread of the general's cruel treatment. Fear ruled the people of the countryside. Holofernes destroyed all the temples and all the sacred groves of the goddesses, for Nebuchadnezzar had commanded that he alone should be worshiped by the people to the west.

The Israelites who lived in Judea heard of Holofernes' approach and were filled with fear. They gathered together to discuss what action they should take.

"He burns all the temples and sacred groves," said one. "What will become of our temple in Jerusalem?"

"It has just been restored," said another. "Surely, the Lord will not allow Holofernes to destroy it."

"We must warn all the nation," said another.

They sent messengers to all the towns of Judea. The towns fortified their walls and stored food and water in preparation for war. The high priest in Jerusalem, Joakim, ordered the villages around Jerusalem to send men into the hill country.

"If we can occupy the passes, we can slow the advance of Holofernes," he said. "It is impossible for more than two men to pass at one time on the paths through the hills. Dig pits in the plains to keep the chariots from advancing."

It was done as the high priest commanded. In Jerusalem, the altar of the temple was covered with sackcloth as a sign of atonement. Men, women, and children dressed in sackcloth and fasted. They prostrated themselves before God and prayed that he not allow the women and children to be carried into captivity, the cities to be destroyed, or the temple in Jerusalem to be profaned.

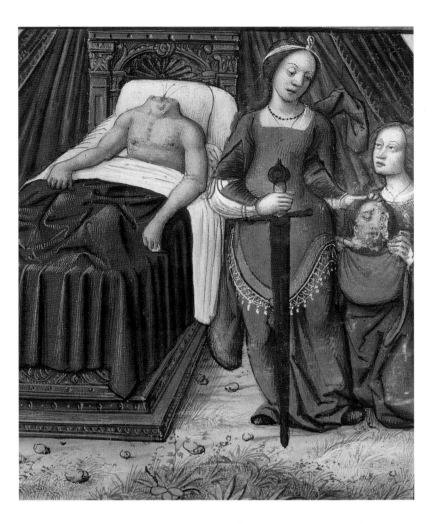

Word of the Israelites' preparation for war came to Holofernes. He was furious. He demanded to know who these people were who dared rise against him.

"These people follow a strong god," said Achior, the leader of the Ammonites, a people living near the Israelites. "If their god is with them, they are invincible. You should leave them alone."

"You speak treason, mercenary," said Holofernes. "You will be punished for your impudence."

He had Achior bound and his troops abandoned him in the hills near the outposts of the Israelites, hoping the Israelites would kill him. But the Israelites untied Achior when they found him and took him into the nearest village.

"Why have you been left here for us to find?" asked the town magistrate.

His advisers then convened. They plotted how to take the hilltops that the Israelites commanded.

"Let us surround them," said one.

"They will soon run out of water and food," said another.

"We can bring them to their knees without putting any of our troops at risk," said a third.

Holofernes agreed. The next morning, the siege of the Israelites began. It went on for days, weeks, more than a month. Food and water became scarce. People grew weak. The men of the towns approached the magistrates.

"We must surrender," said one, "or we shall all perish. Our children and our wives shall perish."

"Courage," said the magistrate. "If we can last just five more days, it will be a sign from God that He hasn't deserted us. Will you agree to endure for five more days?"

They all looked at one another, then at the magistrate. They nodded.

"I angered Holofernes. When he asked about your people, I told him you followed a strong god and that he should leave you in peace. He accused me of treason and left me there for you to find as punishment," said Achior.

"This is a sign from God," said the magistrate. "He is indeed with us. You are welcome among us."

Meanwhile, Holofernes marched into the hills, intending to take the passes by force. He seized the springs, cutting off the water supplies to nearby villages. He camped in the valley, spreading his troops over the valley floor, showing the small Israelite army the strength of his force.

"So be it," said the magistrate.

A local woman, Judith, had been a widow for more than three years, but she still mourned the passing of her husband. She wore mourning clothes every day and remained in the shelter she had erected on the roof of her house.

She was still a beautiful woman, and her husband had left her wealthy with gold and silver, slaves, land, and livestock. No one ever said anything ill of her, for she was a woman of virtue who fasted and kept the laws of the Israelites. When Judith heard of the town meeting, she called the town magistrate and the village elders to her house.

The magistrate and the village elders came quickly.

"How dare you speak as you did today!" Judith rebuked them. "Would you challenge the Lord to prove Himself to you? How dare you give the Lord a deadline! Would you demand that the Lord keep your timetable, or His own? God will not be threatened in this manner.

"We follow the Lord's ways," she continued. "No one worships false idols. How can you possibly doubt that the Lord will protect us against our enemies? The Lord is merely testing us, as he has our ancestors in the past. Is this how we prove our mettle?"

"You are right," said the magistrate. "You are a woman of sound sense, but the people were desperate. They are without water. Pray for us to the Lord. Ask him to send rain to fill the cisterns."

Judith looked at him. "I will take care of this," said Judith. "I will do a deed that our people will remember forever. My maid and I will leave the village this evening. Before the five days are up, through me, the Lord will deliver us."

"What do you intend to do?" asked the magistrate.

"That is not for me to tell you," said Judith.

"God bless you," said the magistrate. "God take vengeance on our enemies."

The magistrate and the village elders left. Judith prostrated herself and prayed to the Lord. When she had finished praying, Judith called her slave woman to her. She took off her widow's clothes, washed off the ashes, bathed, and put on costly perfumes. She combed her hair and pulled it back with clasps of gold. She put on a dress of many colors. She adorned herself with her most splendid jewelry, rings and earrings, bracelets and anklets of precious metals.

She sent her maid for a skin of wine and a flask of oil. She filled bags with some of her last provisions, roasted grain, dried figs, and fine breads. She gave the bags to her maid to carry. They left the village through the main gate. The townspeople were startled to see the change in Judith's apparel.

"I had forgotten how very beautiful she is," said the magistrate to himself. To Judith, he said, "God bless you on your venture."

Judith bowed her head in silent prayer, then ordered that the gate be opened. Judith and her maid went out

and took the path to the valley where Holofernes camped, arrogant amid his army. Judith walked with her back straight, unafraid. Her maid followed closely behind. They walked until they were stopped by Holofernes' sentries.

"Who are you? Where have you come from? Where are you going?" asked the sentry.

"I am from the village of the Israelites," said Judith. "I am running away because the village will fall into the hands of your army and will be destroyed. I am on my way to speak to Holofernes. I have information whereby he can gain access to the entire hill country without losing a single man."

The sentries thought her beautiful. They knew Holofernes would also find her pleasing.

"You've saved your life, woman," said the sentry. "We will escort you to Holofernes' tent. Tell him what you have told us, and you will be safe."

A hundred men surrounded the two women and escorted them to Holofernes' tent. Word spread quickly throughout Holofernes' army of the beautiful woman who had come. The men ran to catch a glimpse of her as she passed.

As they neared Holofernes' tent, the general's bodyguards came forward to greet Judith. They led her into the general's tent, where Holofernes lay in his bed, resting. Netting of exquisite purple and gold, studded with gold, emeralds, and other precious stones, hung around his bed. One of the guards went to him and whispered in his ear.

Holofernes arose and came to greet Judith. Judith knelt before the general. One of the general's slaves helped her to her feet.

"Don't be afraid," said Holofernes. "I have never hurt anyone who has chosen to serve my king. In fact, I would never have attacked your hill people if they hadn't raised spears against me. Now, why have you come to me?"

"Your fame has preceded you, general. I have heard what Achior told you in counsel. You should have listened to him, for he spoke the truth. Our Lord is very strong, and when our people followed His ways, we were invincible. But that is no longer the case. Our people have left the ways of the Lord; therefore, the Lord will deliver our people into your hands through me," said Judith.

"They are without water and food. Because of this, they have chosen to eat things forbidden by our laws. They plan to use the first fruits dedicated to the Lord and the tithes of wine and oil as well. These things are reserved for the priests in Jerusalem. This is an act of sacrilege. I serve the Lord. I will not allow this sacrilege to be carried out."

"You are indeed a wise woman," said Holofernes. "Your God is well served."

Holofernes commanded that food be brought to him. He asked Judith to dine with him. She agreed to stay, but said she would eat only from what she had brought, lest she break the Israelite dietary laws. She stayed in the camp for three days. She told Holofernes that she

OPPOSITE: The story of Judith, the Israelite widow who slew Holofernes, the commander of the Assyrian army, was very popular during the late Renaissance and early Baroque period.

had to pray each night, away from his soldiers, who were not of her faith. Holofernes provided her with a tent of her own. Each night at midnight, she and her maid left the camp, made their way to the river to bathe, and then prayed before returning to camp. Holofernes gave orders to his bodyguards to allow her to pass undisturbed.

On the fourth day, Holofernes told his steward to bring Judith to his tent to dine. Holofernes was filled with desire for the beautiful woman.

"We will drink wine together," said Holofernes. "Tell her to join me."

Judith agreed to come to Holofernes' tent. She dressed in her finest clothes and joined him for dinner, eating only what her maid had prepared and drinking the wine she had brought with her. Holofernes was greatly taken by her beauty. He drank deeply, hoping that she would keep pace with him. Perhaps, he thought, if she had enough wine, she would surrender to his desire.

They ate and drank. Judith sipped her wine discreetly, but Holofernes soon became intoxicated. It grew late. Holofernes' servants withdrew, closing the tent flap behind them. The servants went to bed. Holofernes lurched toward his sleeping compartment, falling into his bed. Judith sat quietly at the front of the tent until she heard Holofernes snore.

She commanded her servant to wait outside the sleeping compartment, then went in to Holofernes. His sword hung upon a bedpost. She took it from its scabbard, and leaned close to be sure he slept soundly. He reeked of wine. Judith prayed for strength as she lifted the sword high above her head, and brought it down hard and swiftly on Holofernes' neck. He made a gurgling sound. She raised the sword a second time and slashed down again, severing his head.

The bedding soaked up the blood. She pulled down the beautiful purple and gold netting and wrapped the general's head in it. She carried the bundle between the curtains of the sleeping compartment and passed into the main tent. She handled the bundle to her maid, who packed it in with the food that they had brought with them.

Judith and her maid left the tent together, walking through the camp as though going to the river to bathe and pray, as was their custom of the previous three nights. But they didn't stop at the river. They walked through the valley, and began the climb to the hillside village whence they had come. When they reached the gates, Judith called out to the Israelite sentries.

"Open the gates!" she cried. "God is with us still!"

The sentries opened the gates and everyone came running to see Judith's return. The sentries lit a fire in order to see one another.

"Praise God," said Judith. "Here is the head of Holofernes, the Assyrian commander-in-chief. The Lord has given him to you through the hand of a woman.

"I swear, the Lord has given him to us, without bringing a blemish to my reputation. I did not sin with Holofernes."

Everyone was dumbfounded. Then, suddenly, everyone talked at once. Judith tried to get their attention. Finally, everyone quieted.

"Take this head and hang it on the battlements. When dawn breaks, every man have his weapons in hand," she said. "Act as though you intend to descend to the valley floor to meet the Assyrians in battle. The soldiers will run to Holofernes' tent, only to find his headless corpse."

They did as Judith commanded. The next morning, the men of the village armed themselves and pretended to head for the valley floor. Holofernes' sentries took alarm. Guards were sent to Holofernes to tell him of the imminent attack. His bodyguard, after getting no answer from the general, entered the bedchamber. He found Holofernes' headless corpse and ran from the tent. He hurried to the tent that Judith

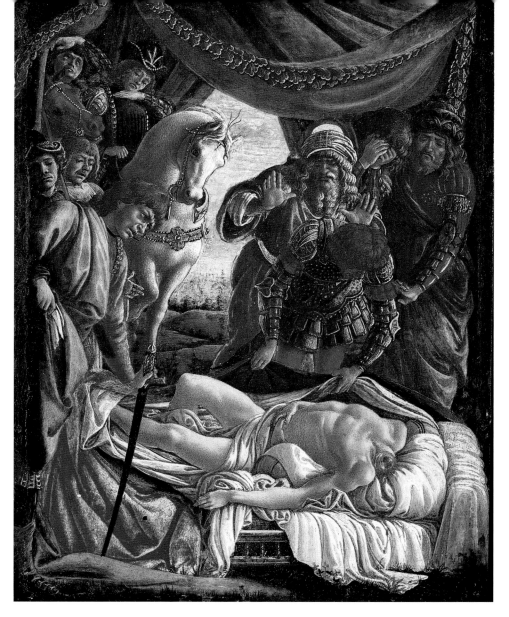

and her maid had occupied. Finding it empty, he hurried to the tents of Holofernes' next-in-command.

"The Hebrew woman has played us false," he raged. "A woman has brought shame upon the army of the Assyrians."

Word of Holofernes' murder quickly spread through the camp. As the soldiers panicked and fled, the Israelites attacked. Word had gone out through the night, so men came from as far away as Jerusalem. The Israelites killed many Assyrians and took possession of the camp, giving Judith Holofernes' tent and all its riches. She took these riches to Jerusalem and dedicated them to the Lord at the temple.

Judith never remarried. She freed her maidservant. When she died at 105 years of age, she was buried with her husband, and there was great mourning in Israel.

CHINA

China has more than three thousand years of written history. The country covers an area as large as all of Europe, and its stories and traditions reflect millennia of cross-pollination with other cultures.

China's pantheon is predominantly male, reflecting a strongly patriarchal society. Before the advent of Buddhism in the sixth century B.C.E., the two major currents of Chinese philosophical thought were Confucianism and Taoism.

Under Confucianism—long the state ideology—women had no rights in the public sphere. They did, however, wield great power as parents in a society that placed a high value on honoring one's father and mother.

Widows could assume their husbands' authority as head of the family. Sometimes they assumed the power of regent for their sons. Many gave up all pretense of ruling as regent and took power for themselves.

How, then, can the stories of the women warriors Mulan and Yinniang be explained? Some speculate that the stories are the product of wishful thinking, although in many times and places, women have disguised themselves as men, especially to go to war. Mulan, for example, assumes a man's clothing and demeanor in order to take her elderly father's place in the Khan's army. The

OPPOSITE: This seventeenth-century painting illustrates court life during the T'ang dynasty of more than a thousand years earlier. The great formality and rituals emphasized the distance between the Chinese emperors and their subjects. As illustrated here, the court encompassed a series of smaller courts, worlds within worlds.

charade is successful until Mulan relinquishes the male role and dons female clothing upon returning to her father's home. The ballad of Mulan was written in the fifth century C.E. The story is Confucian in its outlook: Mulan wishes to serve her father as a son, because her brothers are too young to take his place in the army. In other words, she sacrifices her womanhood to serve her father and the male world.

The swordswoman Yinniang is a different story. The tale, which dates from a written text of the ninth century C.E., may be influenced by Taoism, a philosophical system that sees all of creation infused with spirit. That means that all creatures, animate or inanimate, have a right to existence. The world becomes a magical place. And Yinniang is magical. She is whisked from her father's house and trained by a holy woman, a recluse who trains ten-year-

old girls in a cave in the mountain wilderness. The old woman gives her pupils great magical skills, among them the ability to be invisible. And, invisible to her enemies, Yinniang vanquishes all foes—male and female.

MULAN, THE WOMAN GENERAL

Mulan sat in the doorway of her father's house, weaving at a loom. The shuttle moved back and forth. She was crying softly.

Mulan's father had been called by the Great Khan to enter the army. Her father was getting on in years, and her brothers were still too young to go to war, so neither of them could go in his stead. Mulan worried about what would become of her family if her father were to leave. Who would provide for them?

I am older than my brothers, she thought. It is my duty to take my father's place. It was then that the plan came to her. And with it, the resolution to carry it out.

She put away her weaving and, taking the household purse, went to the marketplace. There she bought a white horse, saddle, saddlecloth, bridle, and a whip. She hid her purchases near her father's house, in an outlying shed.

The next day, the morning star was still in the sky when she crept through the darkness to her hidden mount. She was dressed as a boy—even though she was the eldest of her father's children, she was slight of

unworthy daughter?" she asked herself. The thought brought a tear to her eye. She listened to the night noises—frogs croaking, leaves rustling in the breeze, the river's sighs, owls hooting. She saw a shooting star.

"A good omen," she thought. Soon, she was asleep. The day's travel and the nerve-wracking stress had been exhausting. That night she dreamt of Scythian horsemen in coats of gleaming mail, riding in formation in the wild hills of Yen.

She traveled far the next day, arriving by nightfall at the army's encampment on the Black River. She asked a sentry where she should report. Mulan dismounted and, leading her horse, made her way to the commandant's tent. She saluted and handed him the scroll with the summons to war.

"You are short for a soldier," said the commandant.

"I am short," Mulan said, "but I willingly serve the Khan."

"You have the heart of a warrior," said the commandant, "if not the build, and the clothes of one of her younger brothers fit well. She had build. We will make a good soldier out of you."

The commandant gave her orders, and she bedded down her horse for the night. She washed at the river's edge and made her way to her assigned tent. The eager young men in the tent asked her where she came from. They talked about their own homes. They talked of the glories they would earn in battle. One young man was very pleasing to Mulan's eye. He was friendly, talking about his dreams of conquest. The conversations finally lulled, and sounds of snoring rumbled around her. Mulan lay awake in the dark, wondering if she had done the right thing.

Morning came much too soon. The young men and Mulan spent the day learning the arts of war. They practiced throwing spears and shooting arrows from a moving horse. Time was spent in swordplay. Mulan was an excellent markswoman. Years of weaving and paying attention to fine detail had give her great dexterity.

cut her hair like a man's. She looked like a boy soldier.

Sensing her excitement, the horse trembled under her hands as she smoothed the blanket across his back. She cinched the saddle tight. She put her foot into the stirrup and swung up onto the horse's broad back. She nudged him, and they began their journey.

By nightfall, Mulan had reached the Yellow River. She camped there, beside the river. Even though she was excited at the prospect of her adventure, she was also filled with loneliness. She thought of her father and mother. She imagined them looking for her in the early morning. In her mind's eye, she could see them looking for her throughout the farmstead. She could hear her mother calling her name. They would be perplexed by her absence. "What will they think when they find money missing from the house purse? Will they think me an

"You're very good," said the friendly young man.

"So are you," said Mulan.

Days passed. The young man and Mulan spent their off-duty hours together. He was homesick, as was she. She found herself describing in great detail her life at home. She talked about her "sister," Mulan. The young man wanted to hear all about her. He talked about his home and family. She listened attentively to everything he said. He was an only son, with many sisters.

"It is good to finally have a brother," he said. "I have for so long lived only with women. It's good to be able to talk to another man, someone who can understand fully what I am saying."

"Yes," said Mulan. "I miss my brothers at home. It's good to have a brother close by."

Mulan took great care not to look at him as a woman looks at a man. Instead, she slapped him on the shoulder and poked him in the arm, as men do when talking to one another.

At the end of the day, Mulan was too tired to lie awake long into the night, wondering if her parents missed her. The physical work made her body hard. She slept soundly. She ate as much as the men. She worked

ABOVE: Mulan and her fellow-soldiers may well have looked like these proud warriors of the Eastern Han Dynasty (second century C.E.). OPPOSITE: This gilt-bronze figure of eleven-headed Kwan Yin was fashioned during the T'ang dynasty. She is the Buddhist manifestation of the eight-handed Chun T'i, the Taoist goddess of light and mother of the seven stars of the Ladle (also called the Great Bear).

CHINA

very hard. Not wanting the young men to suspect that she was a woman, Mulan taught herself to walk like a man. It wasn't too difficult—after all, she had many brothers. She learned to brag to fit in.

At last, the day came when the commandant ordered them to mount their horses. The time for battle had come. Her new brother and she rode side by side, traveling many miles through rugged frontier.

"It's exciting, isn't it?" Mulan asked her brother in arms, "to hear the clink of armor, the rattle of saber and drum?"

"I know what you mean," said the young man. "I feel it, too."

When they camped at night, Mulan and her new brother sat in silence, watching the campfires flicker in the darkness. The smell of cooking food and the whinnying of horses filled the air.

"It's a beautiful sight, isn't it?" asked her new brother.

"Yes," said Mulan. "It is."

The next morning, there was unusual excitement as the army started its day's march. The enemy had been sighted the evening before, encamped across the plain.

Orders were carried quickly through the army by messengers from the commandant. The Khan's army marched out onto the plain. Mulan's white horse trembled beneath her.

She could feel his muscles coiling, ready to spring into action. There was a loud crash of cymbals and shouts, and Mulan and her company raced into battle.

As she entered the heated chaos of battle, Mulan reacted as if by instinct. She heard herself shouting. She felt the sword, heavy in her hand, as it split a man's head.

"Help!" her brother cried out.

Mulan wheeled toward his voice. He had been unseated from his horse.

Mulan raced back toward him and pulled him up onto her horse, behind her. Together they galloped through the frenzied fighting, following his frightened horse until they recaptured it. Her brother remounted his horse. They fought together, covering each other's backs. The battle was hard fought, but at last, the Khan's army managed to push the enemy into retreat.

It was only the first of many battles in which Mulan would prove her valor. Always she fought beside her new brother. They were inseparable. Mulan slew many of the Khan's enemies. She fought like a tiger, especially when her brother was in danger. The commandant called her to his tent.

"You are an inspiration to all our soldiers," he said. "You may be small of stature, but your heart is large." He promoted Mulan.

CHINA

141

They fought on through the fall. Winter found them encamped near fresh water and protected from the winds by high hills. The tents were cold at night. The time passed quietly. That spring, Mulan's captain was killed in a skirmish. The commandant called her to his tent.

"You are a tiger in battle," said the commandant. "It is only right that you should be the new captain of your company."

"Thank you, commandant," said Mulan. "I will do my best to make you proud."

Mulan led her men into many battles. She was smart as well as brave. Her men respected their new captain, for she always brought them safely through the battle. Mulan was always in the lead. Her example inspired them to do their best.

Years passed. More promotions followed for Mulan. Her brother in arms also was promoted. Each inspired the other. After seven years, Mulan was elevated to the rank of general. She commanded the entire army. It was then that the Khan's army went on the offensive. She pressed the enemy on every front, using her troops well. It took three years, but, at last, the enemy surrendered. Mulan had been at war for ten years.

"It has been a long time, old friend," said her brother soldier. "Now it is time to return to our families,"

"A long time, indeed," said Mulan. "It seems a lifetime since I stood in my father's house and heard his voice."

"I would very much like to meet your father," said her brother. "I would like to meet the man who sired such a warrior. I would like to meet your sister, too."

"You must accompany me to my father's house," said Mulan. "You will be welcomed to the family as another son."

"I would be honored," said her brother in arms.

Before Mulan left the army for her home, she was called into the Khan's presence. He requested that she bring her staff as well. So Mulan and her comrades made their way to the capital.

"Welcome, General," said the Khan. "I requested your presence so that I may reward you and your men for your dedication and valor."

The Khan gave each a lordship and lands. He gave others prize money.

"What do you want, General? Anything you desire, it is yours," said the Khan.

"I want nothing, your majesty," said Mulan, "except a good horse that can carry me quickly back to my father's house."

"You shall have that and more," said the Khan.

The next day, Mulan headed for home. Her brother in arms and several comrades joined her in the journey. She came to her father's house. Her parents didn't recognize her in her general's cloak.

"Welcome, General," said her father, bowing low. "Welcome to my humble home."

Her father had a servant girl lead her to her old bedroom, which was now a guest room. Her men were taken care of as well. Mulan took off her warrior's cloak and folded it slowly. She opened an old chest and found within it her old dresses.

She bathed and washed her hair. She put on a dress. It felt odd, after ten years, to be so attired. She pulled her hair up with yellow combs and rouged her face. She took a deep breath, then went to join her warrior band.

Her brother in arms looked at her as she entered the room. A strange look crossed his face. He stood to greet her.

"Forgive me for staring, lady," he said. "It is just that you look so much like your brother, for a moment I mistook you."

"You have not mistaken me," said Mulan. "It is indeed I."

Her warriors looked at one another, not believing what she said.

"You are not he," said one.

"Prove it," said another.

Her brother soldier was silent.

Mulan told each a story of his prowess in battle, or of his home—things she had learned in conversation and action over ten years, things that only the general could have known.

"How can this be?" said one.

"How could we have fought beside her all those years and not seen?" said another.

"I see," said her comrade, his eyes warm with admiration. "Our general is a beautiful woman who understands what it is to be a man."

THE SWORDSWOMAN YINNIANG

Nieh Feng, a great general, had a daughter named Yinniang. When she was ten years old, a holy woman saw her and came to speak to the general.

"General, your daughter has great abilities," said the old woman. "I should very much like to complete her education. Please give her to me."

"Who are you, old woman, to demand of me my daughter?" the proud general retorted angrily. "Get out of here, before I have you thrown out."

"Do not threaten me, General," said the old woman. "I shall have what I came for. You cannot keep your daughter from me."

The general had the old woman thrown out of his house. She dusted herself off and disappeared down the street, muttering to herself. That night, the general's daughter disappeared. The general searched the house, and his servants searched the neighborhood, but she was lost.

Five years later, to the day, the old woman reappeared at the general's door with a beautiful girl, her womanhood just blossoming upon her.

"Here is your daughter, General," said the old woman. "She has completed her training."

The old woman disappeared in front of their eyes.

"Is it indeed you, Yinniang?" asked the general.

"I am Yinniang," she said. "Don't you recognize me, father?"

Her mother started crying. Her brothers and sisters kept their distance, suddenly shy. They hardly recognized their once skinny sister with scraped elbows in the poised young woman in front of them. After her mother dried her eyes, she leapt to her feet.

"Enough of this," she said. "You must be hungry after your journey. I'll make all of your old favorite foods."

There was much washing of vegetables and chopping and stirring. While the smell of old, familiar foods cooking filled the air, the general leaned close to Yinniang. Such magic was unsettling.

"Where have you been, daughter? What have you been doing these long five years?"

"The old woman has been teaching me," said Yinniang.

"What has the old woman taught you?" asked the general.

"You won't believe me," said Yinniang.

"I will believe anything after the miracle of your return," said the general.

"She took me to a cave in the wild mountains when she took me from your home. There I found two other young girls, about my age. They had been studying with the holy woman for some time. They could climb like

monkeys. They didn't eat food," said Yinniang.

"What happened then?" asked her father.

"The holy woman gave me a pill and a sword," said Yinniang. "I learned much from the other girls. They taught me how to climb and how to kill monkeys, tigers, and leopards. After some practice, I could throw my sword and bring down hawks and eagles. The sword would return to my hand."

"This is miraculous!" exclaimed her father. "What did you do with this great knowledge?"

"The holy woman took me to a distant city," said Yinniang. "She commanded me to behead a man in broad daylight."

"What did you do?" asked her father.

"I told her that this would be impossible," said Yinniang. "Everyone would see me, and I would be caught and put to death."

"What did the old woman say to that?"

"She told me to have no fear, that no one would be able see me," said Yinniang. "So I crept up on the man and beheaded him in the public square. No one stopped me. No one saw me. I grabbed his head and took it to the old woman."

Yinniang's father rubbed his neck and swallowed. "What became of the head?" he asked.

"The old woman poured a magic brew on it, and it turned into a puddle of water," said Yinniang.

"Is this the only feat that the old woman had you perform?" asked her father.

"No," said Yinniang. "The next year the holy woman took me to a compound in a distant city. She said there was an evil man who lived there and that I was to behead him. By that time, I had learned how to make myself very small, so I squeezed through the crack in the door and made my way into the man's bedroom. He had a small child with him, and I had to wait for the child to leave the room before I cut off the evil man's head."

"But didn't he see you?" asked her father.

"No," said Yinniang. "I hid in the shadows of the rafters until the little child had gone."

"Amazing!" said her father. "The holy woman has made you into the fiercest of warriors. Tell me more of your training."

"The old woman cut open the back of my head," said Yinniang, "and put a dagger there. That way, whenever I need it, the magic dagger is near at hand."

Yinniang's father shook his head slowly. The food was ready, and Yinniang's mother gave out big helpings. That night in bed, the general spoke of his fears to Yinniang's mother.

"Our gentle daughter is no more," he said. "I fear this killing creature that the old woman has returned to us. She can destroy us all, if she chooses."

"She would not harm us," said her mother.

"How can you be so sure?" asked the general. "How do we even know that this creature, this magical soldier, is our long-lost daughter?"

Yinniang acted in a strange manner. Every night she disappeared. Her father didn't say anything to her, nor did he upbraid her for unladylike behavior. In fact, he tried to keep away from her. Her magical powers made him feel uneasy. One day, Yinniang announced that she intended to marry a mirror grinder. Her father didn't protest.

Her mother brought up the matter. "How can a mere mirror grinder take care of our daughter?" she asked the general.

"Look," he said. "Whatever she wants, she can have. I will supply them with a place to live and furnishings and clothing."

After her father's death, the governor of the province sent for Yinniang and her husband, for he had heard of her prowess as a magician and a killer.

"I have a job for you," said the governor. "Liu, the governor of the neighboring province, seeks to undermine my power. I want you to assassinate him. Do you think you can do that?"

"Easily, my lord," said Yinniang.

They soon realized their task wasn't as easy as she had thought.

Yinniang rode a white donkey; her husband rode a black one. Liu, the governor of the neighboring province, was himself a gifted seer. Liu knew of her coming and of the purpose of her visit from a vision. He devised a plan to bring the magician soldier to his side. He sent a messenger to meet her, hoping to convince Yinnian to enter his service.

CHINA

"Greetings, Magician," said the messenger. "The Lord Liu has sent me to bring you to the city."

The fact that Liu had sent a messenger to greet her disturbed Yinniang.

"How did the governor know that we were here?" she asked.

"The Lord Liu is a great seer," replied the messenger. "He had a vision of your approach, and he knows the purpose of your trip."

Yinniang and her husband were nervous as the messenger led them to the governor.

"Your excellency," said Yinniang, "I must apologize for the purpose of my trip. I didn't know that you were a great magician."

"No apologies are necessary," said Governor Liu. "You were only trying to serve your master. What I ask is that you serve me instead. I am deserving of your loyalty."

"It would be a pleasure to serve you, Excellency," said Yinniang.

So it was that Yinniang and her husband came into the service of Governor Liu. After some time had passed, Yinniang sought an audience with the governor.

"Excellency," said Yinniang, "I would ask that you allow me to send a message to my former lord. He has the right to know that I and my husband no longer serve him."

"You are right," said Governor Liu.

Yinniang disappeared in front of him. She returned later that afternoon.

"Look for a woman riding a white donkey and a man riding a black one," Liu told his messenger. "Each will shoot an arrow at a magpie. The man will miss his shot, but the woman will bring the bird down in flight."

The messenger rode until he found the couple. Yinniang's husband aimed an arrow at a magpie sitting in a tree. The arrow missed, and the startled bird took flight. Yinniang nocked her arrow and let fly. The arrow downed the magpie in midflight.

"I have left a strand of my hair tied with red silk on his pillow. My former lord now knows that I no longer serve him. Tonight he will send his woman warrior, Ching-Ching, to kill you. But don't fear, your excellency, I can handle her."

That night in his bedroom, Governor Liu watched two silk ribbons flitting about in the candlelight. One was white, the other red. After several hours, the white ribbon fell to the ground with a thud. Suddenly, the headless body of a woman appeared out of nowhere. At the same time, the red ribbon became Yinniang. She dragged the headless corpse from the room. Outside, in the courtyard, Yinniang poured magic herbs on the corpse, and it turned into a puddle of water. Governor Liu followed her to watch all that she did.

"This was an easy task," she said. "Tomorrow night will be more difficult. My former lord will send his great female champion, Kung-Kung, to destroy you. She is very powerful, and there isn't anything I can do to defend you except to protect your neck with sacred jade."

The next night, Yinniang placed a collar of jade around the governor's neck. She then turned into a small bug and flew up the governor's nose. In the middle of the night, there was a loud sound of metal on stone. Sparks flew from the jade around the governor's neck. Yinniang flew from his nose and resumed her human shape.

"You have nothing to fear from now on," she said. "Kung-Kung will be so ashamed that she has failed that she will never return. She will not want to revisit the site of her greatest failure."

"There is no proof that anyone was here," said the governor. "How do I know that you aren't lying, trying to get a reward from me?"

"You have only to look at the jade collar that you wear, Excellency," she said.

The governor looked closely at the jade collar, and saw a long slice taken from the stone. It looked as though the sharp edge of a sword had cut into it.

Governor Liu was impressed and from then on treated the magician Yinniang with great courtesy. After many years passed, Yinniang came to the governor.

"I ask permission to retreat to the mountains," she said, "to seek a life of contemplation."

"You saved my life," said the governor. "Anything that you desire, you may have."

"I request that you take care of my husband," she said, "for I won't take him with me."

Many years later, Governor Liu died. Yinniang came down from the mountain and mourned at his funeral. Governor Liu's son was appointed governor in his father's place. Yinniang went back to the mountain, from which she never returned.

CHINA

JAPAN

The Japanese myths are recorded in two books: *Nihongi,* which dates from the early 700s, and *Kojiki: The Record of Ancient Matters,* which dates from the late 600s. The stories intertwine historical personages with mythological material. Jingo Kogo is the title of Okinaga Tarashi Hime, the dowager empress who is thought to have ruled in the third century of the common era.

The "land to the west" referred to in "The Empress Jingo Kogo Conquers the Western Kingdom," an area she conquered through miraculous means, has been interpreted as present-day Korea. For centuries, the story served to explain Japan's domination over Korea. Jingo Kogo is still a powerful figure today. Indeed, her likeness is on Japanese currency.

Like women in other cultures, Jingo Kogo assumes power as regent upon the death of her husband. She manipulates her male ministers, promising to assume all blame if the venture to conquer the land to the west fails, and to give them all the credit if it succeeds. She also fulfills the warrior role as a mother protecting her son.

The battles that she fights are with magical creatures, such as a bird man, and with women who plot against her. When the combat is armed, Jingo Kogo, like Scáthach, the Irish woman warrior, has a male champion represent her.

OPPOSITE: Murasaki-shikibu was a Japanese courtier and writer at the turn of the eleventh century B.C.E. Her novel, *The Tale of Genji,* is one of the great classics of Japanese literature. She is one of few famous women storytellers.

THE EMPRESS JINGO KOGO CONQUERS THE WESTERN KINGDOM

Okinaga Tarashi Hime, the daughter of a prince, was young and beautiful. She was also intelligent and shrewd. Most importantly, the gods often spoke to her. Her fame spread to the royal court, and the Emperor Naka-tsu-hiko took her as his empress. Their rule was blessed for nine years, but in the spring of that year, Emperor Naka-tsu-hiko died.

The empress was very sad. She couldn't understand why the gods had so cursed the house.

"Perhaps the emperor angered the gods in some way," she thought. "Why else would they have caused him to die at such a young age?"

The empress ordered all the ministers of the court to search out any sacrilege against the gods throughout the kingdom. She had a special place of worship erected, and, there, a month after her husband's death, she acted the role of priestess herself, overseeing the great purification ritual of the kingdom.

The empress asked the gods to reveal themselves to her and to explain to her how her husband had wronged them. She prayed for seven days and nights to the sound of a lute.

"Why did you take my husband from me at such an early age?" she asked. "How did he offend you?"

At long last, the several gods who had advised the emperor revealed themselves to her: "We told him of the land to the west," said the first god.

"We revealed to him that it contained gold, silver, and gems that sparkle in the sunlight," said the second god.

"We promised him this country," said the third god.

"But he answered us haughtily," said the first god. "He said, 'There is no land to the west. One only has to climb to the mountaintop to see that there is only ocean.'"

"He claimed that we were deceivers," said the second god.

"For that sacrilege," said the third god, "we took his life."

"How can I undo the curse upon the land that my husband's sacrilege has brought about?" the empress asked.

"The land to the west is to be ruled by the child in your womb," said the first god.

"What child is in my womb?" asked the empress.

"It is a son," said the second god.

"You must find the land to the west," said the third god.

"How must I proceed?" asked the empress.

"If you go to seek the land to the west, you must make offerings to all the heavenly deities and all the earthly deities, to all the gods of the mountains, rivers, and seas," said the first god.

"You must create a shrine at the top of the ship for us and put wood ashes into a gourd," said the second god.

"You must make many chopsticks and plates and cast them onto the ocean waves," said the third god.

"Then may you cross the waves to the land of the west," said the first god.

The empress told her ministers to prepare ships as the gods had directed. As preparations were under way, the empress heard of a man who, ignoring her command not to commit sacrilege against the gods, was robbing his neighbors. The man's name was Hashiro Kuma-washi. He was a huge man with large, powerful wings, which allowed him to soar high into the air like an eagle. Because of his great abilities, he didn't think he had to obey imperial edicts.

"This can't be allowed," said the empress. "The gods have commanded, and we must obey. This man will bring down the wrath of the gods upon us all."

The empress put on her coat of armor and took her weapons in her hands. She challenged the bird man to combat on the Moor of Sosoki. They fought long and hard, but as the sun neared midday, the empress struck the bird man a fatal blow.

The empress continued on toward the city of Yamato, for she had heard of a young woman who was plotting with her brother to destroy the empress and the child she carried. The empress put the young woman to death. The rebel's brother, hearing of the death of his sister, abandoned the cause and fled.

Summer approached, and the fleet wasn't yet ready to proceed toward the land to the west. The empress traveled northward, and when she neared the Wogawa

River, she took a needle from her sewing box. She bent the needle into a hook, skewered grains of rice on the hook for bait, then pulled a thread from her cloak. Okinaga Tarashi Hime cast her fishing line into the river and prayed to the gods.

"We are ready to go to the land of the west as you have directed," the empress prayed. "Will we be successful in gaining possession of this land of treasures? Please give me a sign. If we will succeed, let the fish bite upon this hook I have prepared."

There was a tug on the end of her line. She pulled the string in, and, there, caught securely upon her hook, was a trout.

The empress ordered sacrifices made to the gods. She commanded that a rice field be set aside for them. She tilled it herself, and to irrigate the field, she dug a channel from a spring on the hillside, but a great rock stood in the way. She tried to cut a channel through the rock, but it wasn't possible. She offered a sword and a mirror to the gods and prayed that they would split the rock. There was the rumble of thunder, and a bolt of lightning struck the rock, splitting it in two.

The ships were ready, but as yet there was no army. The empress made her way to the seashore and looked westward across the sea.

"Following the instructions of the gods," she said, "I will go to the land of the west myself and personally oversee its taking."

She waded into the water.

"May the gods part my hair if I will be successful," she said.

She dove into the waves. As she arose from the sea, her hair parted. The empress wound it upon her head in the fashion of men. Okinaga Tarashi Hime turned toward her ministers.

"War is an undertaking not lightly made," she said. "Should we fail, the blame will be put on you, for I am a woman. Therefore, I will assume responsibility for our venture. I will dress like a man, and I will speak as a man. The gods of heaven and earth will guide me.

Should we succeed, you, my ministers will receive all the credit. If we should fail, I alone will be to blame."

Her ministers bowed low. They swore to follow her commands. The empress ordered all able-bodied men to come together to form an army and to practice the arts of war. No one assembled.

"This is the will of the gods," she said to her ministers. "I must erect a shrine to the gods and offer to them a spear and a sword."

She did so, and the troops gathered. It was now time for the empress to give birth. She inserted a white stone into her vagina and prayed.

"Let me not give birth to my son until the day I return from conquering the land to the west," she said.

Her labor pains ceased. The ships were prepared for sail. As they sailed toward the west, a favorable wind came up behind them. All the fish of the sea came to the surface and bore the ships on their backs toward the land to the west. The waves, too, bent their backs to carry the ships. The empress' navy didn't stop until the waves carried her ships halfway across the land to the west.

The king of the land to the west spoke to his ministers: "This must indeed be a divine presence," he said. "How else can you explain the coming of their ships in this manner?"

His ministers agreed. The king carried a white flag to the empress and prostrated himself before her.

"I will obey the emperor," he said to the empress, thinking her a man. "Every year I will send many ships with tribute to your land."

Okinaga Tarashi Hime acknowledged his oath.

BELOW: As Jingo Kogo, Okinaga Tarashi Hime might have used splendidly crafted arms such as these. OPPOSITE: A nineteenth-century B.C.E. Japanese banner by Utagawa Kunisada represents the empress Jingo Kogo and her minister.

She stood her staff at the king's gate, showing that she accepted him as a vassal. She then returned to Japan. Her son was born in the village of Ito. While she had been gone, men had plotted to take the throne from her and her son. Prince Osi-kuma and his brother Kago-saka decided to kill the newborn prince. They went into the wilderness, looking for a sign from the gods as to whether their venture would be successful. A huge boar attacked them and ate Kago-saka, but his younger brother, ignoring this omen, proceeded to lay a trap for the empress and her infant son.

Meanwhile, the empress, knowing of the plot, sought to throw Osi-kuma off the trail. She decked her ship as a funeral ship, hoping that he would think the infant had died. She hid troops below deck. The ruse worked long enough for her troops to swarm ashore and take the troops of Osi-kuma by surprise. The two armies fought hard. At last, the general of the empress' troops sent word to Osi-kuma that the empress had been killed and that he would surrender. At the same time, he ordered his men to replace their swords with wooden replicas and to hide their real swords close by. He had them hide extra bowstrings in their topknots. They then marched to surrender to Osi-kuma. They cut their bowstrings in front of Osi-kuma and his troops. They threw their wooden swords into the sea.

Osi-kuma fell for the trick and ordered his men to stand down, unstring their bows, and put their swords away. At that very moment, the empress' general ordered his men to retrieve their hidden weapons and to restring their bows with the bowstrings hidden in their hair. The empress' men destroyed the army of Osi-kuma, and Osi-kuma drowned trying to flee by swimming across a nearby lake.

The empress held the throne for her son until he was old enough to take over. He ruled for many years, and his reign was marked by peace. The empress, his mother, lived to be one hundred years old.

INDIA

The culture that created the *Rig Veda*, the first Hindu sacred text, emerged from an Indo-European–speaking people, Aryans who invaded the Indus River valley and much of the Mediterranean area two thousand years before Jesus was born. In India, they settled in the Punjab region around 1500 to 1200 B.C.E.

Goddesses have been an integral part of Hindu mythology for millennia. However, in the *Rig Veda*, the earliest scripture, the goddesses are of lower stature than the gods, with a few exceptions. The great goddesses of modern Hinduism, such as Parvati, Durga, and Kali, aren't even mentioned in the text.

In India, the invaders found local gods and goddesses, who in time influenced and infiltrated the conquerors' pantheon. The major goddesses of Hinduism became more prominent than they had been in the *Rig Veda* during the period when India's great epics were composed, 400 B.C.E. through 400 C.E.

One of the great warrior goddesses, Durga, comes to the fore in artwork and literature beginning around 400 C.E. The great warrior goddess Kali is a relative latecomer: the first reference to her dates to 600 C.E. In some stories, Durga, assembled from body parts made by the other gods, can from herself create the awful goddess Kali, whose name means "the dark one." Kali has the power to destroy

OPPOSITE: Durga is the warrior avatar, or incarnation, of Shakti, the Hindu mother goddess. As Kali, she is the gruesome dark goddess of death. Traditionally, Durga radiates an aura as yellow as the sun; in this eighteenth-century B.C.E. painting, the aura has become a golden crown.

the world and subdue Siva (Shee-va), the fearsome god of destruction and regeneration.

Durga and Kali are avatars, or incarnations, of Shakti, as are Sati and Parvati, who are both wives of Siva. Sati is Siva's first wife, who commits suicide because her father, in an act of disrespect, did not invite Siva to a great feast.

Parvati, whose name means "she who lives in the mountains," is the reborn Sati. In one story, Siva, her husband, makes fun of dark-skinned Parvati by calling her "kali." Parvati then tries to shed her dark skin. Through fasting, prayer, and ritual, she succeeds in getting a golden complexion. The dark skin she sheds becomes the goddess Kali.

Although Durga is mentioned in the Vedas—the four canonical collections of hymns, prayers, and liturgical formulas of which the *Rig Veda* is part— she isn't yet the great warrior

of later mythology. Her job in the later mythology is to battle demons who threaten the very cosmos. Durga rides a lion into battle, resembling in this the Egyptian goddess of war, Sekhmet. She is, in one divine aspect, connected with the fertility of plants, but she is fed with blood offerings, liquor, and meat, much like the Egyptian goddess Hathor.

Durga, like the Greek goddess Athena, is born from the gods themselves. Each god creates a part of her and gives her a weapon, because only a woman warrior can destroy the demon Mahesa, who has subjugated them.

ABOVE: This fifteenth-century painted wood statue from Trivandrum represents Kali, the dread goddess of death and vengeance, and one of the avatars of Shakti. RIGHT: The goddess Parvati cuddles her infant son, Ganesha, the elephant-headed god of wisdom. OPPOSITE: Kali's skull necklace is stylized in this eighteenth-century painting.

DURGA BATTLES MAHESA

Unlike the Amazons of Greek and Roman stories, Durga isn't destroyed by her male opponents. Just as in the Greek and Roman stories, her adversaries fall in love with her, but she destroys them, as in the story "Durga Battles Mahesa."

The demon Mahesa performed many heroic deeds in ancient India, and as a boon was made undefeatable by the gods. The only way he would ever lose a battle was to be bested by a woman warrior.

INDIA

Because there was no such thing, this did not worry him. This was a great gift indeed.

The demon Mahesa waged a relentless war against the gods until in the end he prevailed. He took their places, and they retired to the mountains in defeat and anger. The vanquished gods sat and stared at one another. The ignominy of defeat made their faces burn with shame. Indignation filled them with such anger that they radiated heat and light.

The heat and light they gave off grew together until it was a huge ball of fire and light. From the ball of light came the body of a beautiful woman. She had no features, so Siva gave her a face. Yama gave her hair. Vishnu gave her many arms. When she was complete, the gods gave her weapons.

Siva gave her a trident, Vishnu gave her a discus, Vayu gave her a bow and arrows, and Himalaya gave her a fierce lion to ride into battle. Durga took the gifts of the gods and raised her voice in a great roar that shook the very heavens. She went to the field of battle then and challenged the demon Mahesa.

"Girl, you are too fragile to fight," said the demon.

"Are you afraid to face me?" she asked.

The demon laughed. "You are too beautiful to wage war."

"I challenge you," Durga said steadfastly.

"Where is your male protector, my dear?" asked the demon, with mock solicitude. "Surely you haven't come here alone?"

"I need no protector," said Durga. "Will you face me in battle?"

"I would indeed face you, my dear. Close up," said the demon. "Cease these warlike words. I can teach you words of love."

"I come here to do battle," said Durga. "I shall destroy you."

"Come here, little one," said the demon. "I shall teach you the ways of love."

At that, Durga charged the demon fiercely. Mahesa backed up in surprise at the fury of her onslaught. At first he laughed, but then her great strength surprised him. Throughout the day they fought as the blazing sun passed overhead. Mahesa wearied and he grew worried. He tried changing his form. He charged her in the form of a great buffalo. But the lion that Durga rode bit and clawed him, and the warrior goddess slashed at him with her ten arms, which wielded the ten weapons of the gods.

Mahesa became an elephant, towering over Durga, but she kept pressing forward and slashed at him again with her ten arms. Finally, Mahesa became a giant with a thousand arms. Durga urged her lion mount to the attack. The lion leapt, knocking Mahesa the demon to the ground, and Durga thrust her great lance through his heart.

Thereafter, she was known and honored as Mahesa–mardini: the slayer of Mahesa the demon.

BELOW: As in many societies, the image of an aristocratic lady making music stands for civilization and order. Here, a lady plays a vina to a parakeet.

RIGHT: Durga, astride her lion mount, kills the demon Mahesa, thereby putting an end to the unrelenting war he waged against the gods. Some say that the shape-shifting Mahesa would ultimately have defeated the gods themselves, were it not for the fierce goddess' ten arms and ten divine weapons.

WOMEN'S TALES, WOMEN'S VOICES

Women warriors, the Amazons in particular, have intrigued writers and artists since time immemorial. They were popular subjects from the Renaissance on, as Classical themes were rediscovered, perhaps evoking in some male artists and tellers of tales a wistful desire for a time when men did not rule. The Amazons, remnants of another age, were believed to have lived on the outskirts of the civilized world, and were sometimes identified with the lost realm of Atlantis. In the early 1500s, *Las sergas de Esplandián*, a hugely popular romance by the Spanish novelist Garci Rodríguez de Montalvo, described "California," an island in the ocean inhabited by women resembling the ancient Amazons. European explorers traveled across the Atlantic expecting to find the lands of these valiant women—lands, not incidentally, reputed to be "rich in gold and precious green stones," as another source says.

In the mid-1960s, with the winds of radical change blowing, a stylish British series made its way across the Atlantic, and suddenly on North American television there was a woman of action—on the side of the angels. Mrs. Emma Peel, as played by Diana Rigg, was not only intelligent, articulate, and cool, but she said what she thought and had a pointed sense of humor. She was expert in the martial arts and things scientific. She displayed two revolutionary

OPPOSITE: Women warriors of mythology reflect women warriors in fact. Paradoxically, Mary, Queen of Scotland and France, has acquired legendary status because of the very human drama of her story, and because she went head to head with one of history's great warrior queens, Elizabeth I of England and Ireland. This miniature, painted by a contemporary, François Clouet, emphasizes Mary's intelligence, as well as the wit and charm for which she was both admired and reviled.

MARIE
REINE
ESCOS
ss

qualities. One was that she was unapologetically herself, and the other was that she did not define herself by a relationship (or lack of one) with a man. There was a husband somewhere, probably to keep her relationship with Steed from turning gooey, although the audience was teased with hints about the nature of her partnership with Steed anyway. Whatever the case, she went toe-to-toe with Steed as much as with the bad guys, and sometimes saved him from the bad guys, too.

That there could be an audience for Peel indicated that her qualities resonated with a number of people, no doubt women and men both. But in 1969 an odd thing happened. Mr. Peel—not dead, it turned out, just long lost—reappeared, and Mrs. Peel disappeared, to be replaced by Tara King, a more traditionally feminine character. Like Altamont following only months after Woodstock in that same year, the reaction to the feminist revolution was already setting in.

Emma Peel was descended from some of the women in the stories you have just read, and from a number of other sources as well, including Wonder Woman and other comic-book heroines. The comics, of course, have traditionally borrowed their structure— the epic, eternal struggle between good and evil—from the ancient myths, and Wonder Woman, a devotee of the Greek goddesses and gods of Olympus, did so explicitly.

Perhaps what happened to Peel was that she was acceptable as a token capable, independent woman, but that society (or at least the show's sponsors) lost its nerve when more women began to resemble her, when the myth she tapped into proved too powerful. Or perhaps so many women were now like her that her myth had merged with reality, and so ceased to be.

In the 1970s, half a century after women won the vote, the so-called second wave of feminists (the ancient myths show a far longer struggle), twentieth-century Amazons, led the fight for personal autonomy—which often came down to legal battles for physical integrity and fair wages. Words were demythified: "girls" were once more very young women, not mature females afraid of aging, and the word "ladies," with its upper-class connotations, was retired.

Women—and girls—explored history and myth, finding there, as I had, models of effectiveness and wisdom. The Great Goddess, whether Isis, Hera, or Juno, was rediscovered, and Wonder Woman came to television. Originally introduced in All Star Comics in December 1941, Wonder Woman—curiously enough—was a brunette in the era of power blondes like Mae West and Carole Lombard. An Amazon who answered to the Olympian goddesses, her power was literally contained by her outfit, a cheesecake version of heroic nudity, designed to make her unthreatening to the primarily male audience of the comics. On television in the second half of the 1970s, she pre- sented a double message: It's okay to be effective, just remember that your attractiveness comes first.

Twenty years later, many girls and women expect both to express their womanhood and be taken seriously. At the same time, it is the nature of Amazons both to be outlaws and to fight on their sisters' behalf. The latest manifestation, Xena, the Warrior Princess, brings to life a combination of many a little girl's fantasy (and probably not a few boys'); she is as much a descendant of Emma Peel as of Wonder Woman.

The most enthralling modern tales, from Star Trek to Star Wars, have been explicitly inspired by myths, but we are bombarded by contemporary myths—worldviews—from books and television shows, commercials and other advertisements, popular and classical music. Each day we make our way through labyrinths of suggestion, associations, and preconceptions that go straight to our unconscious.

For every tale retold for millennia, a thousand others have been lost. The sons of the Greek women lived in the women's quarters until they were seven years old; perhaps it is they who told the stories they heard as the women spun wool and wove it into timeless patterns. But perhaps, like housebound Amazons, the women kept certain tales and songs for the girl children, part of the women's mysteries that we will never know.

The "Song of Deborah" is attributed to the Deborah of the Book of Judges whose story has been told here. There is a respected scholarly theory that the *Odyssey* was written by a woman, possibly Nausicaa, a princess who rescues Odysseus in the epic. This theory is supported by the separateness of the worlds of ordinary Greek women and men: no man of the time would have had the detailed knowledge about the women's sphere that brings the epic poem to life. (By the same token, the passages dealing with ships and other traditionally masculine areas are often vague, even shaky.)

It is a judicial axiom that it is not enough that justice be done, it must be seen to be done. The magician's greatest feat is to make his assistant disappear, but in the women's realm, the greatest

achievements are those that make women visible. Women must not only perform the deeds, taking up our power as responsible actors in the world, but we have to tell our stories, learn the sounds of our own voices. It is no coincidence that the heroine of our age, at the cusp of the new millennium, is the Persian Scheherazade, who took back the night, saving her own life and that of her sister by weaving irresistible tales for one thousand and one nights.

BELOW: The Belgian-born artist Médard Tytgat captured the compelling enchantment of Scheherazade's storytelling. Her spell has captivated a slave as well as the misogynist sultan Shahriar.

BIBLIOGRAPHY

Anderson, Bonnie, and Judith Zinsser, eds. *A History of Their Own: Women in Europe from Prehistory to the Present*, Vol. 1. New York: Harper & Row, 1988.

Bach, Alice. *Women, Seduction, and Betrayal in Biblical Narrative*. Cambridge: Cambridge University Press, 1997.

"The Ballad of Mulan." In *The Temple and Other Poems*. Translated by Arthur Waly. New York: Alfred A. Knopf, 1923.

Boccaccio, Giovanni. *Concerning Famous Women*. New Brunswick, N.J.: Rutgers University Press, 1963.

Bolen, Jean Shinoda. *Goddesses in Everywoman: A New Psychology of Women*. New York: Harper & Row, 1984.

Budge, E. A. Wallis. *The Gods of the Egyptians*, Vol. I. Chicago: Open Court Publishing Co., 1904.

Cavendish, Richard, ed. *Legends of the World*. New York: Crescent Books, 1989.

Christie, Anthony. *Chinese Mythology*. London: Hamlyn House, 1968.

Cross, Tom Peete, and Clark Harris Slover. *Ancient Irish Tales*. New York: Henry Holt and Company, 1936.

Diner, Helen. *Mothers and Amazons: The First Feminine History of Culture*. New York: Julian Press, Inc., 1965.

Diodorus Siculus, Vol. 2. Translated by C.H. Oldfather. Cambridge, Mass.: Harvard University Press, 1933.

Eisler, Riane. *The Chalice and the Blade*. New York: HarperCollins, 1987.

Ellis, Peter Berresford, *Celtic Women: Women in Celtic Society and Literature*. Grand Rapids, Mich.: William B. Eerdmans Publishing Co., 1996.

An Encylopedia of World History: Ancient, Medieval and Modern, Chronologically Arranged, 3d ed., revised. Edited by William L. Langer. Boston: Houghton Mifflin Co., 1963.

Erman, Adolf. *Life in Ancient Egypt*. New York: Dover, 1971.

———. *The Literature of the Ancient Egyptians: Poems, Narratives, and Manuals of Instruction, from the Third and Second Millennia B.C.* New York: E. P. Dutton and Co., 1927.

Fraser, Antonia. *The Warrior Queens*. New York: Vintage Books, 1990.

Godolphin, Francis R.B., ed. *The Greek Historians: The Complete and Unabridged Historical Works of Herodotus, Thucydides, Xenophon and Arrian*. New York: Random House, 1942.

Grammaticus, Saxo. *History of the Danes*, Vol. 1 and 2. Translated by Peter Fisher. Totowa, N.J.: Rowman and Littlefield, 1979.

Green, Miranda, ed. *The Celtic World*. New York: Routledge, 1995.

Gregory, Augusta. *Lady Gregory's Complete Irish Mythology*. New York: Smithmark Publishers, 1996.

Grimal, Pierre, ed. *Larousse World Mythology*. New York: G. P. Putnam's Sons, 1965.

Hallo, William W., and J.J.A. van Dijk. *The Exaltation of Inanna*. New Haven: Yale University Press, 1968.

Hamilton, Edith. *Mythology: Timeless Tales of Gods and Heroes*. New York: Mentor Books, 1969.

Harrison, Jane Ellen. *Prolegomena to the Study of Greek Religion*. Princeton, N.J.: Princeton University Press, 1991.

Homer. *Iliad*. Translated by Robert Fitzgerald. Garden City, N.Y.: Doubleday & Co., Inc., 1974.

Homer. *Iliad*. Translated by E. V. Rieu. New York: Penguin Books, 1950.

Homer. *Odyssey*. Translated by E. V. Rieu. New York: Penguin Books, 1946.

Hooke, S.H. *Middle Eastern Mythology: From the Assyrians to the Hebrews*. New York: Penguin Books, 1991.

Isocrates, Vols 1 and 2. Translated by George Norlin. New York: G. P. Putnam's Sons, 1928.

Kinsley, David. *Hindu Goddesses: Visions of the Divine Feminine in the Hindu Religious Tradition*. Berkeley: University of California Press, 1988.

Kleinbaum, Abby Wettan. *The War against the Amazons*. New York: McGraw-Hill Book Co., 1983.

Kramer, Samuel Noah, ed. *Mythologies of the Ancient World*. Garden City, NY: Anchor Books, 1961.

———. *Sumerian Mythology*. 2nd ed. New York: Harper & Row, 1961.

Kojiki. Translated by Donald L. Philippi. Tokyo: University of Tokyo Press, 1968.

Larrington, Carolyne, ed. *The Feminist Companion to Mythology*. London: Pandora Press, 1992.

Lofts, Nora. *Women in the Old Testament*. New York: Macmillan Co., 1949.

MacCana, Proinsias. *Celtic Mythology*. London: Chancellor Press, 1996.

March, Kathleen, and Kristina Passman. "The Amazon Myth and Latin America." In *The Classical Tradition and the Americas: European Images of the Americas and the Classical Tradition*, Vol. 1. Edited by Wolfgang Haase and Meyer Reinhold. New York: Walter De Gruyter, 1994.

McEvedy, Colin, *The Penguin Atlas of Ancient History*. New York: Viking Penguin, 1967.

Morford, Mark, and Robert J. Lenardon. *Classical Mythology*. New York: David McKay Co., 1974.

The New English Bible with the Apocrypha: Oxford Study Edition. Oxford: Oxford University Press, 1976.

Nihongi: Chronicles of Japan from the Earliest Times to A.D. 697. Translated by W.G. Aston. New York: Paragon Book Reprint Corp., 1956.

O'Rahilly, Cecile. *Táin Bó Cuailnge*. Dublin: Dublin Institute for Advanced Studies, 1976.

Patai, Raphael. *The Hebrew Goddess*, 3d ed. Detroit: Wayne State University Press, 1990.

Phipps, William E. *Assertive Biblical Women*. Westport, Conn.: Greenwood Press, 1992.

Pintchman, Tracy. *The Rise of the Goddess in the Hindu Tradition*. Albany: State University of New York Press, 1994.

Plutarch. *Lives*. Translated by Bernadotte Perrin. New York: Macmillan Co., 1914.

Pringle, Heather. "New Women of the Ice Age." *Discover* (April 1998): 62–69.

Smyraeus, Quintus. *The Fall of Troy*. Translated by A. S. Way. New York: Macmillan Co., 1913.

Spence, Lewis. *Myths and Legends of Ancient Egypt*. London: George G. Harrap & Co., Ltd., 1949.

Spretnak, Charlene. *Lost Goddesses of Early Greece: A Collection of Pre-Hellenic Myths*. Boston: Beacon Press, 1992.

Sturluson, Snorri. *The Prose Edda*. Translated by Arthur Gilchrist Brodeur. New York: American-Scandinavian Foundation, 1929.

The Táin: From the Irish Epic Táin Bó Cuailnge. Translated by Thomas Kinsella. Oxford: Oxford University Press, 1969.

Traditional Chinese Tales. Translated by Chi-Chen Wang. New York: Columbia University Press, 1944.

Tyrrell, William Blake. *Amazons: A Study in Athenian Mythmaking*. Baltimore: Johns Hopkins University Press, 1984.

Virgil, *The Aeneid*. Translated by Rolfe Humphries. New York: Charles Scribner's Sons, 1951.

Waldherr, Kris. *The Book of Goddesses*. Hillsboro, Ore.: Beyond Words Publishing, Inc., 1995.

Warner, Marina. *Monuments and Maidens: The Allegory of the Female Form*. New York: Atheneum, 1985.

Wilford, John Noble. "Ancient Graves of Armed Women Hint at Amazons." *New York Times*, February 25, 1997, C1.

Wolkstein, Diane, and Samuel Noah Kramer. *Inanna: Queen of Heaven and Earth*. New York: Harper & Row, 1983.

PHOTOGRAPHY CREDITS

Art Resource: pp. 141, 142, 146, 149; ©Alinari: pp. 2, 125, 126 (Regione Umbria); ©Erich Lessing: pp. 5, 8–9, 15, 20, 21, 22, 40 bottom, 43 bottom, 46–47, 50, 51, 55, 56, 66, 68, 72, 74, 75, 76, 77, 80, 81, 89, 102, 105, 106, 109, 112, 118, 123, 130, 131, 138, 140; ©Giraudon: pp. 6–7, 16, 37 left, 45, 48, 83, 84 top, 91, 94, 95, 100, 129, 137, 139, 143, 145, 152, 153, 162 top, 164 right; ©Scala: pp. 12–13, 14, 25, 26, 30, 40 top, 58–59, 61, 70–71, 73, 78–79, 84 bottom, 88, 92, 93, 96–97, 98, 133, 134, 135, 156; ©Werner Forman Archive: pp. 23 (British Museum, London), 52–53, 103, 114–115 (National Museum, Copenhagen), 120 (Musees de Rennes); ©Nimatallah: pp. 42, 44, 57, 65, 69, 101; ©SEF: pp. 62–63; ©Cameraphoto: pp. 85, 128; ©The Pierpont Morgan Library: p. 127; ©Victoria & Albert Museum, London: pp. 147, 157, 165, 166–167, 169; ©Borromeo: p. 164 left

©Christopher C. Bain: p. 110

©Christie's Images: pp. 31 bottom, 32, 37 right, 43 top, 49, 60, 67, 99, 161, 171

E. T. Archive: pp. 33, 151, 154; ©Archeological Museum Naples: p. 11; ©Archeological Museum, Aleppo: p. 17; ©Christies: p. 19; ©Egyptian Museum Cairo: p. 27; ©Louvre, Paris: pp. 28–29, 36; ©Archeological Museum, Florence: p. 31 top; ©Civic Museum Udine: p. 39; ©Prenestino Museum Rome: p. 90; ©British Library: p. 162 bottom; ©Victoria & Albert Museum: p. 163

FPG International: ©Tom Craig: pp. 34–35; ©Harold De Faria Castro Cast: p. 41; ©Telegraph Colour Library: pp. 86–87; ©Keren Su: p. 144; ©Dennis Cox: p. 148; ©Travelpix: p. 155; ©Jean Kugler: pp. 158–159

Leo De Wys: ©George Munday: p. 117

North Wind Picture Archives: pp. 108, 111, 113, 116, 121, 122

Stock Montage, Inc.: ©Charles Walker Collection: p. 107

Siena Artworks/©Michael Friedman Publishing: 119

INDEX

A

Achilles (Greek hero), 43, 54–56, 76, 77
    and Penthesilea, 78–79, 79–81
Aeneas (Roman hero), 84
    and Dido, 89–95, 91, 94
    in Latium, 98–103
Aife (Irish woman warrior), 106, 112–116
Ailill (Irish king), 118–121, 119
Allecto (Roman goddess), 99–100
Amata (Roman queen), 99–100
Amazons, 14, 54–81, 55–58, 66, 67, 72
    fascination with, 168
    queen Hippolyta, 64–67
    queen Myrine, 56–61
    queen Penthesilea, 56, 76–81, 78–79
    Rubens' painting of, 70–71
    and Scythians, 68–74
Amphora, 40, 67
Andromache (Trojan heroine), 77
Antiope (Amazon queen), 67, 74–75
Aphrodite (Greek goddess), 39, 84. See also
    Venus
Apollo (Greek god), 41–43, 46–47
Ariadne (Greek heroine), 73
Armor
    Celtic, 108, 109, 112, 113
    Japanese, 156
    Sumer, 23
Artemis (Greek goddess), 38, 47, 48. See also
    Diana
Athena (Greek goddess), 17, 38–40, 40, 42, 44,
    74, 84. See also Minerva
    birth of, 38, 51
    and Paris, 39, 43
    in Trojan war, 43, 48–51, 77

B

Bacchantes, See Maenads
Bastet (Egyptian goddess), 37
Bible, women in, 15, 124–135
Botticelli, Sandro, paintings by, 15, 92, 134, 135
Bridget (Irish goddess), 120

C

California, as Amazon land, 168
Camilla, 98–99, 101–103
Celts, 104. See also Irish mythology
    armor of, 108, 109, 112, 113
Chinese mythology, 136–149
Chinese women, 137, 139, 143, 145
Clouet, François, painting by, 169
Coliseum (Rome), 86–87
Comics, women in, 170
Confucianism, 136
CúChulainn (Irish warrior), 106, 107–108
    and Aife, 112–116
    and Morrigu, 120–123
    and Scáthach, 109–112
Cybele (Anatolian goddess), 61, 61
Cyrene (Libya), Roman ruins at, 62–63

D

Danu (Irish goddess), 105, 114
de Montalvo, Garci Rodriguez, Las sergas de
    Esplandián, 168
Deborah (Biblical character), 124, 126–127
Defour, Antoine, painting by, 129
Delilah (Biblical character), 15, 126
Delphi (Greece), 41
Diana (Roman goddess), 11, 84, 98, 98. See also
    Artemis
Dido (queen of Carthage), 85, 88–95, 91, 95
Durga (Indian warrior goddess), 160–163, 161
    battle with Mahesa, 163–165, 166–167

E

Egyptian mythology, 24–37
Eis (Irish bird-headed woman), 113, 116
Eleusis (Greece), Sacred House in, fleeing
    maiden from, 68
Enki (Sumerian god), 20–23
Eos (Greek goddess), 49
Epona (Irish goddess), 122
Etruscan women, 82, 101
Euripides, 56

F

Fergus (Irish king), 106, 118–120, 122
Finnabair (Irish woman), 106

G

Ganesha (Indian god), 162
Gentileschi, Artemisia, painting by, 125
Gorgons, 58–60, 60, 99
Greek mythology, 14, 38–51, 54–81
Greek women, 50, 52–53, 54, 68, 69
Gundestrup Cauldron, base of, 106

H

Hathor (Egyptian goddess), 16, 25, 26, 26, 30, 31,
    34
    and Re, 32–37
Hector (Trojan hero), 76, 77
Hephaistos (Greek god), 48, 51
Hera (Greek goddess), 14, 14, 38, 39, 40, 40. See
    also Juno
    and Herakles, 64–67
    and Trojan war, 45–51
Herakles (Greek hero), 64–67, 65, 67
Hestia (Greek goddess), 84
Himeji (Japan), castle in, 158–159
Hindu mythology, 160–165
Hippolyta (Amazon queen), 64–67
Holofernes (Assyrian general), 128–135, 135
Horus (Egyptian god), 35

I

Iliad (Homer), 10, 38, 40
Inanna (Sumerian goddess), 17, 18, 20–23
Indian mythology, 160–165
Indian women, 165
Irish mythology, 14, 104–123
Isis (Egyptian goddess), 24, 27, 33, 36, 37
    and Re, 26–31
Isis (Roman goddess), 84
Isthar, See Inanna

J

Jael (Biblical heroine), 124, *126*, *127*, *130*
    freeing Israel, 126–128
Japanese mythology, 150–157
Jezebel (Biblical character), 126
Jingo Kogo (Japanese empress), 150–157, *154*, *157*
Judith (Biblical heroine), 15, 124, *125*, 126, 128, *129*,
    133, *134*
    slaying Holofernes, 128–135
Juno (Roman goddess), 84, 85, 100. *See also* Hera
    and Aeneas, 89, 93, 99
Jupiter (Roman god), 89

K

Kali (Indian warrior goddess), 160–162, *162*,
    163
Kwan Yin (Chinese goddess), *141*

L

Las sergas de Esplandián (de Montalvo), 168
Li Lung-mien, painting by, *145*
Libyan Amazons, *See* Amazons
Lilith (Sumerian goddess), *19*
Loughcrew (Ireland), *107*

M

Maenads, *81*, 96–97, 100
Mahesa (Indian demon), 163–165, *166–167*
Mary (Queen of Scotland and France), *169*
Medb (Irish warrior queen), 14, 106, 118–121,
    119
Medusa (Greek monster), 60
Mesopotamian relief, *21*
Minerva (Roman goddess), *12–13*, 83, 84, *84*, 85.
    See also Athena
Morrigu (Irish goddess), 106, 121–123
Movies, women in, 15–17, 168–170
Mulan (Chinese woman warrior), 136–143
Murasaki-shikibu (Japanese woman storyteller),
    151
Myrine (Amazon queen), 56–61

N

Nebuchadnezzar (Assyrian king), 128, *131*
Neith (Egyptian goddess), 24–26
Nephthys (Egyptian goddess), *37*
Ninshubur (Sumerian woman warrior), 22–23

O

Odyssey (Homer), 10, 38, 171

P

Palma, Jacopo, the Younger, painting by, *128*
Parvati (Indian goddess), 162, *162*
Peel, Emma, 168–170
Penthesilea (Amazon queen), 56, 76–81, *78–79*
Poseidon (Greek god), *46*
Priam (Trojan king), *76*, *76–77*

R

Ramses II, sarcophagus of, *28–29*
Re (Egyptian god), 24, 26–37
Rig Veda (Hindu sacred text), 160
Roman mythology, 82–103
Roman women, *84*, 84–85, *90*, *101*
Rubens, Peter Paul, paintings by, *45*, *70–71*, *95*,
    98

S

Sati (Indian goddess), 162
Scáthach (Irish woman warrior), 106, 109–116
Scheherazade (Persian woman storyteller), 171,
    171
Schliemann, Heinrich, 56
Scythians, 68–74
Sistrum (Egyptian instrument), *31*
Siva (Indian god), 162, 164, *164*
Spranger, Bartholomaeus, painting by, *130*
Sudan, relief in, *33*
Sumerian mythology, 18–23
Sun wheel (Ireland), *111*
Syria, marble head of woman from, *20*

T

Táin Bó Cuailnge (The Cattle Raid of Cooley),
    107
Taoism, 158
Tara (Ireland), *117*
Theseus (Greek hero), 74–75
Thetis (Greek sea nymph), 43–44
Tintoretto, Jacopo, paintings by, *12–13*, *85*
Trojan war, 41–51
    queen Penthesilea in, 76–81
    scenes from, *43*, *45*, *75–80*
Troth (Egyptian god), *37*
Turnus (Roman warrior), 99–103

U

Uathach (Irish woman), 106, 111–112

V

Venus (Roman goddess), 84, *92*, *93*. *See also*
    Aphrodite
    and Adonis, 89
    and Aeneas, 88, 90–93
    birth of, 15, *88*
Vesta (Roman goddess), 84
Vestal, statue of, *103*
Virgil, *Aeneid*, 84, 89–95, *91*, *94*, 99–103

W

Wonder Woman, 170

X

Xena, the Warrior Princess, 170

Y

Yakshini (Indian goddess), *164*
Yinniang (Chinese woman warrior), 138,
    144–149

Z

Zeus (Greek god), 38, 40, 51
    and Trojan war, 41–51